The Runemaster Chronicles

The King of the Dead & The Sinister Brand

Robert Peterson

Illustrated by Kory Fuhrman
St. Wilfrid Press
Miami

St. Wilfred Press

Miami

First Edition 2023

10 9 8 7 6 5 4 3 2 1

Copyright © 2023 Robert Peterson

All rights reserved.

ISBN: 979-8-9877373-2-3

Library of Congress: 2023905099

Now Available

By Robert Peterson

Viking Mania
Selected Stories of Kings and Queens,
Gods & Ghosts
Vols. I & II

Ragnar Lothbrok
Sea King
The Untold Story

A Narrative Account of His Death
& The Revenge of His Sons

Available on Amazon

Dedication

Dedicated to my ancestors of western Norway, including Peter Jenson, 1834-1879, whose widow Synneva Nilsdatter, 1838-1910, emigrated to Stoughton, WI with her family, including her son Johannes Peterson who would later marry Anna Bjornson whose father was born in the County of Buskerude, Norway. Their son Sanford would become my paternal grandfather.

Dedicated to my ancestors of eastern Norway. Anna Evensdatter, 1860-1944. Born in Grimstad, Norway, emigrated to Scandinavia, WI, Waupaca County. She married Thorvole Rise, 1862-1897, who was born in Froland, Agder County, Norway. Their daughter Josie was my maternal grandmother.

Table of Contents

List of Illustrations 1
Preface 2
    About Runemasters
Chapter One 8
    By the Light of the Hairy Star
Chapter Two 43
    To the King's Court
Chapter Three 67
    The Death of a Courtier
Chapter Four 101
    Dead Men Talk & The Sinister Brand
Chapter Five 115
    The Neo-Necromancer
Chapter Six 145
    The Careful King
Epilogue 150
Prologue to Vol. II 154
    The Jutland Cannibal
Suggested Further Reading 161
About the Author 162
    Robert Peterson

List of Illustrations

The Family
Steinson
Astra Storm Queen
Bormo
Jarl Hakon Harefoot
Map of the North
The Neo-necromancer

Preface

About Runemasters....

It was the year 606 of the common era, but only a handful of religious clerics knew it. Most of them were in Rome with plenty of other things to keep them occupied; the new pope, Savinianus, was mired in unresolved doctrine battles as well as being worried by the Lombards and imminent famine. He resolved these issues to the satisfaction of nobody, and his tenure as the leader of the Church of Rome was seen as a disaster compared to his predecessor Gregory the Great.

The ordinary people reckoned the years by the reign of the King; if asked the year you were born in, for example, you might reply, "I was born in the fourth year of the reign of King Tofa Addleson."

But there was great confusion over who ruled what on the Island of Zealand, so one must assume there would have been difficulty in the reckoning of years: if anyone lived long enough to care.

In the port city of Roskilde on the island's west side, King Hugleik the Stout held sway over that part of the island and several other islands nearby. However, Harald Rattson, Jarl of Haugen, an important city directly across the water from the southern tip of Sweden, also claimed the throne. His claim was made stronger by his bloodless capture of the rich Island of Falster to the south and dozens of nearby smaller islands. A third contender, Eadgils the Usurper, House of Yingling, waited for the outcome of the eventual battle between these two titans, but he was assassinated by his nephew, leaving the whole country in turmoil. Such was the political situation of the most populated region of the north. Sometimes things got better for a while, but kings and their hungry sons ravaged and raided to the disadvantage of everyone but their poets, called skalds, who made a good living writing dishonest poetry that made the guilty look virtuous.

However appalling this lack of chronology would be to modern people, it didn't interfere with the appetites of either Gudgaest Hammer-Hand (also known as *Gudgaest Ox-Back,*) or his guest *Gunner the Bold.* Later Gunnar would be known to history as *Gunnar the Bald,* but at this time, he was not yet thirty and still had hair on the top of his head.

They were sitting in a large farmhouse ten miles inland from the port of Roskilde. This farm, which looked from a distance like any other, had two remarkable features; the first was a workshop, where blocks of stone were carefully stacked in a corner under tarps awaiting the Runemaster's attention. The second was that it had chimneys, both for the workshop and the main house.

These were the only chimneys to be found in the north at this time, and if Gudgaest hadn't seen them in use while employed as a member of the Imperial Guard in Byzantium, there wouldn't have been any.

Homes at that time had a central fire pit that provided the sole source of heat for both warmth and cooking; the smoke they produced, which was a lot, was vented by a small hole in the ceiling. So, there was a lot of smoke, especially in the winter. These irritating fumes were added to by lamps that burned tallow, which, of course, produced as much smoke as light. Only wealthy landowners could afford to spend money on candles. However, in this particular home, the oil lamps were fueled by shark liver oil that burned much cleaner.

As the men laid waste to a platter of fried bread, a serving woman brought them another dish of breaded flounder and another of garlic pottage. Then, she brought in another pitcher of mead for the third time.

"I just got a commission to carve a stone for your old friend Snorri the Raider," Gudgaest said in between mouthfuls, "he died when he went to beat a slave for being lazy."

"He was always beating people," said Gunnar as he wiped his mouth on his sleeve. "But by Loki's pate, there were many who would pay good silver to give him a beating. He was the worst raider in history, and that's saying a lot."

"He was certainly incompetent," agreed his friend as he reached for more fish, "he was too cheap to hire a local guide when he raided one of the coastal towns of the Franks, he got stuck on a sand bar, and as his other ships were trying to pull him off it the Franks sent their own ships out to fight him. Half his men died, and he didn't get a single silver coin."

"It was worse the year he raided the Rus," said Gunnar as he reached for the mead, "he left too late in the year, and with contrary winds, he took weeks longer than usual to get there. By then, raiding season was over, and he had to return or face getting trapped by the ice. After that, he raided no more; nobody would sign with him."

"Well, I'll find something good to say on his stone; one dead man's silver is as good as the next."

"I hear your son is a father," said Gunnar.

"Yes, Jens has a son named Arn after my father, the babe and his mother are doing fine; they tell me he has a mop of dark hair just like his father did when he was born."

"Has he the sight?"

"Jens says so, a strong one too, he claims. How it will show itself, time will tell. I told him to leave the service of Jarl Rattson, no matter how much silver he has given him. He should take his family and join us here on my farm; we have plenty of room. There will be fighting soon, and I know not if his magic will be enough to keep him alive. He is a warrior with a strong mind, but a dozen wild dogs can kill even a seasoned fighter."

"I agree," said Gunnar as he pushed himself away from the table, having devoured enough food for three men, "he should go north to the Geats; they could use a Runemaster there; you've heard the same stories that I've heard. Fools are trying to resurrect the dead; it's more than just rumors; I've read the signs."

"It's risky business trying to bring these shades back; ravers are impossible to control. Take my word; nothing good will ever come of it. But you are right; those who can wield the power of runes to protect a warrior's grave are in high demand. Jens should lay aside his spear and take up the chisel. But of course, that is for him to decide."

"I wonder who is responsible for this rank insanity of raising spirits? Where can such magic be found?" asked a perplexed Gunnar.

"It's not to be found among the lore of Odin, he alone can talk with the dead, but yet he does not raise them although he tried to, in a roundabout way, with his son Baldur. No such magical innovation has ever been successfully used among Runemasters; this I know for a certainty. Yet here it is, a mystery, a very dark and evil mystery."

"No doubt this mage will reveal himself to us at some point. Somebody seeks power in stealthy and arcane ways. Before this mischief is done, a lot of trouble will be caused. It will come to grief in the end; such things always do. The only question is when this savant of evil will show himself?"

"You speak sooth, my friend," said Gudgaest as he mulled over his drink, "in the end, whoever wields this power will come forth to use it. What claims he will make and what he has to back up his authority remains to be seen. I've told Jens about this; all who wield magic should be on their guard lest we become entangled in this evil affair. It's possible he's not a Runemaster; after all, we are not the only ones who have found the power of the earth."

"But if it is a Runemaster, he might fall victim to the fate of Otar Skallafesterson."

"Ah, yes," Gudgaest sighed as he recalled the tale of a Runemaster who had died ten years ago, *"Otar the Fool.* He certainly was an idiot; he was attempting to raise a corpse to find where it had buried a hoard of gold and silver. Yet it came to nothing. Either he was inept in reciting the spell, or the spell betrayed him; I'm not sure which."

"Well," said Gunnar, "in a way, he did *raise* the corpse. I would pay good silver to have seen the look on his face when passersby came clamoring to his door to report that he had a dead man on his roof. That must have been hard to explain. No wonder he ended his days among the Rus."

"He was certainly inspired when it came to getting in trouble. Did you hear about the scandal he caused when he carved the runestone for the warlord of the Geats, no? Let me tell you about it," Gudgaest said after draining a cup of wine, "He was bribed by a rival family to cut runes that said scandalous things about the deceased warrior, including the charge that he buggered the bottoms of young boys when he wasn't busy applying his lips to the cock of a horse. He didn't think they would ever know the difference, but eventually a man who could read runes saw the stone and reported it to the local Jarl. A ship was dispatched with orders to find and kill the author of this blasphemous text. Otar found out in the nick of time. He prudently took ship to west Scandia where he stayed for several years."

"By the hammer, he was rightly called the fool," said Gunnar as they both laughed heartily at the discomfiture of the foolish Runemaster.

"We must be vigilant then and keep our eyes open. We can't count on this man, whoever he is, to be as inept as Otar was. And I hope that my son and grandson will come to no harm in the battles that are sure to come."

Gudgaest's hope for the continued good health of his son and his family was rewarded, for he took no blows during the contest, but the same could not be said for Jarl Rattson, who was ambushed and killed by his enemies one night as he rode to his farm. Jens grabbed his family and wasted no time in fleeing for their lives. Yet sorrow did come to his life during the time of upheaval, for not long after this, his wife died in a mishap, leaving him to raise a young boy by himself.

After a number of adventures and narrow scrapes, he found employment among the Rus as an advisor to a warlord, eventually marrying the man's widowed niece. He prospered both in love and in his employment for the next five years, leaving only when the man died of a fever leaving his lands to his eldest son, who disliked all Danes. Jens returned to Daneland, taking employment under an important Jarl of Falster, who gave him leave to practice his given trade of rune cutting. His fame spread, and by the time he died, he was wealthy and greatly respected by all who knew him.

His son Arn took up the trade when he was hardly more than a boy. His magical ability was a question mark, yet he worked diligently alongside his father for some years before Jens died peacefully, which was a wonder considering that he was often in the very vortex of strife during those turbulent times.

If his magical ability had yet to be measured, Arn showed himself as a keen student of the past and a sharp observer of the present. But being a savant of the wild magic the runes embody was often a harbinger of severe tests and harrowing adventures. Yet it had always been so since

Father Odin, while hanging on the Tree impaled by a spear, snatched the runes for himself. He paid a heavy price for his knowledge; even long after this event passed into legend, the use of runes still demanded payment, but not always in the same coin.

All Runemasters in Arn's line strove to use the rune magic for the benefit of the society in which they lived, and he was no exception. But the world was changing; it was getting bigger every year, and new religions took hold in some places. This caused certain of the wise to be concerned; if the Old Ones didn't get their due, what would the result be? Nobody knew, not even the seers of Uppsala nor the Sammi mages of the far north. Unknown powers probed the land while others, with cool and calculating minds, took a close look at the world of the north and the strategic importance of Danevold. Yet there was hope, Baldur Bjornson was now High King among the Danes, and he drew to him the best and brightest in the land. Dark powers will always work to supplant the good, but in the port city of Roskilde, a new power was growing that gave all good people hope for the future. Trade flourished under the new king, who, although a mighty warrior, favored trade over raiding and encouraged artisans of every stripe to come to practice their trade under his protection. The north flourished, a fact not lost on hostile forces.

Time: Early 7th Century C.E.
Place: A small village fronting the Bay of Mecklenberg on the Baltic Sea coast south of Denmark

Chapter One
By the Light of the Hairy Star

One of spring's surest and most welcome signs is the year's first commission. This afternoon a boat arrived from the Island of Goats, near the coast of the Geats, just a few days' sail due north of us across the narrow sea. It was an easy project to start on, with no magic, just a small stone to commemorate the death of an old chief. The terms were decent enough, A small leather bag with a fold-over flap with a clasp and shoulder strap. It was worked in a fanciful representation of the God Vik, half-snake, half-dragon; three small crocks of honey--always welcome for the strong drink I brew. And a few dozen forged fishhooks of different sizes. There was no gold or silver; these were the wrong sort of people for that kind of thing.

I took their leader and his man on horseback to the hillside a few miles away, where I get most of my rock. There was layer upon layer of dark cream-colored stone that could be, with enough effort, pried loose and broken into convenient sizes. Stones were littering my little quarry from previous years and unsuccessful efforts. I bade them choose a size; I will return with some of my workers tomorrow and cut a new stone from under the ground. Fresh stone would be needed; once exposed to the air, the surface became hard and brittle, difficult to cut runes into. Their selection was somewhat dictated by the boat size they came in. Also, they were interested in a memorial to a loved one, not a heroic pillar to honor the final resting place of a warrior.

One of the most persistent myths about those who carry magic is that they lead frugal lives and live alone, as some Christian holy men do. I don't know whence this came, but it is a falsehood. I have denied myself no lawful comfort and see no value in self-denial. My grandfather Gudgaest kept a large table, and so did my father Jens when he was able to. While I do not consider myself to be their equal, especially of

Gudgaest, who was the mightiest user of magic in many generations, or my father, whose strength of character was admired by all who knew him, I nonetheless follow their custom and always have a house full of children, relatives, and visitors or as in the present instance, customers.

On the way back, I heard much from these men. There was talk of war and raids, which in itself was not remarkable. Indeed, it would have been a great surprise if it had been otherwise. Yet their conversation was entertaining, especially when Rolfer, the older of the two and in charge, described the fate of a pirate raiding vessel that had come to plunder them but instead found a new and permanent home on the broken-bank shoal just outside their harbor. The people of Goat Island took a gruesome glee in seeing these raiders struggle for their lives only to be swept away by the strong current, never to be seen again.

"But you know, Master Arn," he said as he looked uneasily over his shoulder, "there is news from Scandia; evil things are said to be happening in the north. Things that should be dead aren't staying dead. It is said that there are monsters abroad."

At this, he quickly clasped his hand into a fist three times in a row, a warning against enchantments. Halfbarth, his man or friend, I couldn't tell which, made no such sign, yet he grabbed at the small charms he wore around his neck and muttered something to himself. I noticed one of them was Thor's hammer which most people, including myself, wear. But I saw something else, a cross; I had seen in Rus this death sign so venerated by the Christians. But it was not common there and, in these parts, rarely seen. Yet here it was. I thought this man was careful, taking no chances; he felt the need for all the protection he could get.

"There are always monsters in Scandia, just as there will always be raiders. Perhaps a woman troll is looking for a husband. Are both of you married?" This jest brought out smiles, but a look of concern stayed in the eyes of both.

"I do not know what is happening, but a refugee from Scandia was washed ashore a few weeks ago. He had been driven mad by the unnatural things that he saw. He made a raft of tree limbs tied together thinking that he could cross the narrow sea in something like that," said Halfbarth shaking his head. "I didn't talk to him myself, but those who did question him heard a tale so evil that their faces turned white."

"That is unwelcome news," I replied, "your people are pale enough after a long winter. But mayhap your hidden reefs will do you more service, and the fog too. I've heard it said that the mists sometimes cover your island for days. What will become of this man?"

"We will keep him; we do not harm those who come to us for no bad purpose. Yes, the ocean might help us keep safe, and the fog too. But the deep mists might not hide us from those whose eyes are already dead." After this chilling thought, the conversation faltered, and we rode in silence for a while.

There was little life in the village as we rode through it; only a few dogs noted our presence. The men and boys would still be in the fields planting; at this time of year, no daylight could be wasted.

"Do you not fear raids? You have no walls," asked Halfbarth."True, we have built no walls yet, but we can easily be missed by those who sail the coast; our little harbor has a narrow inlet screened by several tiny islands. From the west, I said, pointing, "we have little to fear. The land beyond our fields is rugged, with deep gullies and steep hills. Beyond that are wild tribes of no name. East of us, there are rivers and lakes that would be more trouble than we are worth to cross and, of course, the Danes to the North who are now, as you have told me, fighting each other again despite having a new king. From the south, there is a ring of hills; they can be crossed, of course, but so far, the Thurgians and other tribes have left us alone; perhaps they think that the ground here is as bad as the forests in that area that go on for mile after mile; nothing but stunted pine trees and piss-burrs, all worthless." As we rode through the gate of my estate, it was the same as the village, virtually deserted, with only one old man butchering a sheep to be seen. Once we entered the dwelling, though, there was plenty of activity. Women bustled to and fro carrying firewood, buckets of water, and jugs of mead from the storehouse. As we came through the door, I was mobbed by my children, three of them anyway. Gudrin, 14, the eldest, was helping her mother, but her sister Helga who was almost eight, grabbed onto my legs and squealed. Her brothers were full of questions pestering the newcomers with all manner of inquiries about life on an island. Flosi, 12, wondered why islands didn't sink. His brother Kanute, 10, told him it was a dumb question that almost started a fight. I put them both to the task of watering the horses.

After entering the house, Halfbarth called down an unusually long and complicated blessing of the Gods upon it and all within. Thankful as I was for this, I remembered what my father said about people mainly being religious when threatened. Devotion to the Gods often meant that the howl of wolves are heard.

Astra was resplendent in her deep blue tunic that covered her tall and angular form. We made a contrasting pair; she was tall, not much shorter than me; she was fair, long-limbed, and had deep blue eyes, whereas I have a medium build with dark hair and eyes; I'm exceptionally strong, although I don't look it. By trade, I might be a cutter of stones and a giver of life to runes, yet I was brought up well-trained in the arts of sword, axe, and shield. Astra is my Goddess, an almost timeless one. Life and children had yet to leave a line upon her face; I married her young, she had only celebrated fourteen years when we took the sacred vows that bound us together. I considered myself a man of the world, twenty-two years old at that time, yet I had much to learn. Tonight, her swept-back blonde hair positively shimmered in the light of the fire and oil lamps. She wore the gold and amber necklace I was given years ago for services to a king who ruled far to the east in Rus, where I had lived with my father. I never told anyone its worth; it's never wise to call attention to things of great value.

Tonight we enjoyed a meal of fish and duck with a spicy garlic pottage. This and bowls of my best mead made us all very merry.

Besides my visitors from afar, a few of my neighbors stopped by out of curiosity. One of them, Lief Thorson, a weaver, was a natural conversationalist and storyteller. He had a rich store of anecdotes, some very bawdy, others intriguing and funny. After telling us about a cuckolded farmer whose wife did more in the shed than milk the goats; that is, until her long-suffering husband caught them and sliced open her lover's liver with a scythe, he told us a very different sort of story.

"A day after the new moon, I met my man Herold who was to pay me for the cloth he sold to the Danes. This he did, for he is a dependable man. Then he told me of a rumor among the Danes that all is not well in Scandia and that traders are being warned to go only to the coast, not inland. I heard this from several different people. While none of the stories agreed with each other, there was one common thing; a shield wall, they said, no matter how strong, cannot withstand the onslaught of those who are already dead. I know nothing, yet this is what was being said. This seems beyond reason, but according to Herold, this was what was being said. He also said that the main port of the Danes, Roskilde, had been fortified, this time with stone walls. They used the old wall for firewood," he noted dryly.

Talk of the supernatural will always wander; before we finished, we discussed the wolf riders that had been seen a few years ago far to the south of us, men who were not content to ride wolves but turned into wolves themselves. And mention was made of the deadly sprites who posed as comely women in order to lure farmers from their fields where they would be slain and roasted for an unholy supper.

"Nothing but mischief comes from leaving your field for any woman," said Thor Nilson, the warrior turned farmer who had sat in the corner so quietly that I forgot he was there. "And I, for one, would be very suspicious of a beautiful woman wandering around by herself in these parts. The Gods gave us good soil and water but didn't do us any favors where the women are concerned. You got the only good-looking one within a three-day march of this place," he said, nodding at my wife. "Nor should the old adages about leaving a field for anything, I mean anything, without taking your sword and shield with you, be forgotten. Death by man and beast and fiery demons has always been common enough. Evil creatures and robbers walked these fields and forests since the days of our first fathers."

*

In the morning, I went forth in the wagon with two men to get a stone to work on. I took my bag of wooden wedges along, metal wedges would have been much easier to work with, but I couldn't take the chance that I would inadvertently touch a stone that I would later need for an enchantment. Even a slight touch of iron on a stone would prevent a spell from forming or, worse, change the content of the spell entirely.

That afternoon we muscled the stone from the wagon onto the bench in my workshop. There, with a cup of mead in hand, I gave thought to the project before me. It was simple enough; a group of friends made a small hill over the grave of a respected elder and wanted to mark it with a stone. None of them could read the words that I will carve; not one in a hundred could do that, but no matter. For generations to come, the mere sight of this stone would speak words of respect, honor, and love to people regardless if they were lettered or not.

As I sat there thinking about the probable design I would use, I felt the catlike feet of Astra enter behind me. My workshop is a large room with three big windows, and two doors, one of which led to our sleeping quarters, the other to a gravel drive; it also had benches for friends and idlers who sometimes came to see my work. As the largest landowner and the richest person in the district, I am expected to offer hospitality to all who show up at my doorstep. Indeed, our gate is the last to be locked at night.

"Have you decided what to say?" Astra said, looking at the stone.

""Oh, something short and to the point, I would think. I'll put a bird on the back, maybe an egret or an eagle. Red paint for the front runes, blue for the back. Or maybe dark green."

"Is something going on up in Scandia? Or is this just another wolf-man scare?"

"That I can't say," I replied, handing her my cup of mead, "there is no doubt their concern is genuine. There are always unquiet spirits, bloodsuckers, and sprites nipping at the heels of the living," I said as I arranged my tools on the table. "My father saw my grandfather defeat the necromancer."

"Your grandfather used a battle axe, as I remember it. But your father never said much about this famous battle. I recall him talking about it years ago, just after we had met. But I never understood what that repulsive man wanted."

"He wanted what too many others in history have wanted; power, more power, and more power. Power can be like a thirst, one that can't be quenched. It becomes a disease that can't be cured." I replied, "You're right, though, there is much I don't know, and perhaps my father didn't know either. My grandfather kept many secrets for all of his great and loud talk and tales."

"Do you think that your grandfather really split the mad magician's head open with an axe? Fighters always boast and brag so much it's hard to tell what's real."

"You can depend on it," I replied. "Nor was it grandfather's first effort in that regard. Remember, he was a bodyguard to a Rus prince when he was young. The Rus only hire the best who have experience; they can afford to."

"How long will it take for you to finish this?" she said, looking at the stone, "I feel a storm coming."

"I'll be done with it by nightfall tomorrow. Will that be soon enough?"

I didn't expect an immediate answer, and I got none. Her mind would travel to whatever place it went to learn the likely future of storms. If one were coming, she would know; if one were needed, she would make it. After a few moments, I laid aside the chalk and turned to look at her. I could see the color returning to her eyes as she stood there as still as one of my rune stones. She was a tall woman of singular beauty despite her sharp features and high forehead. Her eyes were like the deep freshwater pools that sometimes one will encounter on the fringe of a forest. When she casts her mind forth to the other place, the change in her eyes was a little unsettling; they grew grey and cold as a winter's morning. I couldn't help thinking how different she was from the local women who tended to be dark and short with broad faces. Nobody knows where she came from; she was an orphan whose mother was found at the point of death by an old couple who lived near the village. It was assumed that this woman survived a wreck with her child. Nobody knows more; for myself, I think she came from across the narrow sea. Blue eyes are more common there, as are women who can master the weather.

"They had better leave by Woden's Day," she said at length, "there is a storm coming out of the east, a strong one. They need to be home by then."

"That gives us four days; they'll be ready to leave first thing the day after tomorrow."

"If you say so," she said doubtfully, looking at the unmarked stone. She started to say more, but at this point, the steward asked about putting the sheep in the south meadow, which took her away for the time being. I thought it was just as well; I needed to make the stone chips fly. I grabbed the sax, which was just a hatchet with a specially ground edge for cutting letters, and my wooden mallet; with my eyes on the chalk marks, I set to work.

The following afternoon our two guests were in my workshop to inspect the finished work I had propped upright. The back depicted a stylized eagle painted a bright blue. All in all, it was a fine example of cut-stone art. The men were obviously impressed.

"Master Arn, this is wonderful. The old man would have smiled for an entire moon if he were here to see this. But tell us," asked Rolfer as he bent down to view the runes, "what these letters say, we cannot read them." At this, his friend chuckled and offered his opinion that there wasn't a soul on the whole island who could make sense of this.

HERE LIES RAVIN THE STALWART SON OF SIDAR * ALL LOVED HIM * THIS STONE WAS RAISED BY HIS FAMILY AND FRIENDS AND CARVED BY ARN SON OF JENS * WODEN TAKE HIS SOUL

These words were colored in red ocher, which contrasted sharply with the natural tint of the rock. How long the paint would last is unknown, but if I had to say I would venture a guess that it would outlast the life of anyone now living.

The next morning Thor and I accompanied the finished stone through the village to our little harbor where we shared a last cup of wine with Rolfer and Halfbarth. After the stone was hoisted aboard the two men set sail to take advantage of the land breeze and were soon on their way. Over the past few days, I had become somewhat fond of them. Somehow, they seemed a bit more than could be expected from an island of goat herders. Last night we again talked again about the goings-on in the north. These men were not given over to foolishness nor were they the type who were easily frightened; their words made me uneasy.

The promised storm on Woden's day came and blew itself out doing no real damage for all of its noise and bluster. I decided to give my eldest son Flosi a day off from farming to go fishing. Every fit male in the region was now toiling in the fields with few exceptions. So if you wanted fish, you either got them yourself or went without; there were no fish to be bought anywhere. Flosi had been taken in hand by our steward who was teaching him the rudiments of running a large farm. I had ten hides of good land besides pastures and wood-lots. The term *hide* of land is imprecise; it refers to how much land can be plowed by a team of oxen in a day. All teams were not equal, nor was the ground. Still, I had plenty of land, a dozen good workers, their families, and a few slaves. I prefer freemen to slaves since they work harder and are more trustworthy. My slaves were inherited, taken as children from a slaver's pen in the land of the Danes by my father, who took pity on them for being so wretched.

We used a skiff in the harbor that I used to pole around the shallow waters. I took the fishhooks recently given me and tied them to a line, one hook for every arm's length of twine. We baited the hooks, tied the far end to a flat, round rock anchor I had carved a hole in, and laid the line perpendicular to the shore. The other end I kept in the skiff; I tied it to a piece of log just in case it got dropped overboard. Then we sat down and waited, munching on some fried bread I brought.

As for my son Flosi, I didn't know what to make of him. If he had magic, it was well hidden. But magic was capricious; it ran strong in some lines only to skip a generation or stop altogether. Time alone would reveal whether or not any of our offspring had the gift. Flosi seemed intelligent enough; he had friends, yet he was a bit of a loner given to solitude at times. Thus, his personality favored his mother more than mine. Physically he was not much different from other boys his age. He was quick, agile, strong, and had good eyesight. His hair was sandy, reddish brown, which seemed to be getting lighter in color the older he got.

As we sat and talked, Flosi suddenly looked up at me and asked, "What was it like, the first day you knew you had magic? How did you know? Were you waiting for it?"

"I certainly wasn't waiting for it; I was no older than you the first time. I knew very little about it really."

"Did you call it? Mom told me once that she could call a storm. Can she really do that?"

"Your mother has some very strong powers. But no, I didn't call it. In fact, it was a day very similar to this; I was waiting to go fishing with my father. This occurred back in the village we used to live in, south of here. I've told you about that, I think."

"You told me about living in a poor village that stank of mud."

"Right, it was named **Mud Village**, as I told you before, my father was a councilor to a Dane noble who fell from favor and a war club to his head; we were forced to flee in a hurry. Father felt that going to a quiet backwater might be healthy, so we went to a clan of outcast Swabians. Yes, there was mud; the local potters dug out clay and threw the overburden wherever they felt like it. If it rained hard enough, it washed into the village and made an unholy mess." Here I paused to take a pull of mead from the flask.

"As I was saying, we stopped on the riverbank to eat when I saw a bunch of skulls mounted on sticks nearby. These were the skulls of a band of murderers that had tried to rob the village a year earlier. They failed to reckon with the advanced notice that a wary seer on the run, my father, could give. When they showed up, they were killed by the local men who put the skulls up as a warning. Innocently enough, I went over and touched one," I said with a sour laugh.

"But a skull can't hurt you, can it?" Flosi asked, looking up at me.

"It didn't kill me, but it scared me out of my skin; infernal beasts protect me from every being that scared again! One moment I was standing next to the river; the next, I was looking out from *INSIDE* a skull. It felt like everything between my ears was boiling. Then, in a flash came things about this man's life. How he lived, and what it was like to die. It was no great pleasure either, I can tell you that. I felt the rock that knocked out his front teeth before he got the arrow in the belly. I heard him rage and tasted his blood. He was a foul beast of a man brought into this world by other beasts just as bad. I slept for two days after that, weak as a kitten. My mother was gone by then, but my father's new woman took care of me. Father opened his mind and heart after that, and I learned much. As for the village of smells and mud, we left soon after and traveled to the Rus, where my father got another position, this time as an adviser to a warlord."

At this point, my lesson in family history was disturbed by the arrival of a broad skiff filled with wooden fish traps. "By the nine-Hels," I whispered, "it's Big Ears Dold ." The wonder was not in seeing this man, a common occurrence, but that he was calling to us. He was famous for his ability to remain silent in any language you'd care to name. He was called old, but that was problematic; he was of those who looked old from the day they grew their first whisker. He lived in the village's worst hovel, which was a feat considering the state of some dwellings.

"Good day to you, Master Arn, and your young lad. I be headed past the surge to plant my traps, the hammer save me when I see ye here a-fishing. So, I do come most humbly to ask your thinking on the hairy star that's come. Two nights now, I've seen it when I got up to piss. Bright as the bald spot on Loki's pate, I think."

"I have not seen it. Where away is it?"

"Look to the western sky; it was up a good way. Looked red to me. But see for yourself. It's a foul and bad omen, I warrant. Tidings of evil from the trickster or worse. I don't have to tell you that a hairy star seen this month means no good for us; it's a warning."

"You could be right," I said, making a mental note to see this for myself tonight, "thanks for telling me." At this, he nodded and plied his pole towards the outlet to the sea.

"By Thor, that was very strange, strange indeed," I said, marveling as I saw this lean retreating figure.

"A hairy star sounds strange," my son observed with a puzzled look.

"Maybe, but not as strange as this old fool talking to me. He hasn't said a word since I stitched up his hand from a turtle bite four seasons ago. Your mother will probably think that I made this up. Oh, and a hairy star is just that, a star that looks like it has hair, or at other times a tail as it moves across the sky, a little farther every night. It might mean everything or nothing; I won't know until I see it if it's there. Ungbens drinks a lot, not always the best stuff either."

Later that afternoon, we made our way triumphantly home with buckets full of fish for the Sea God had favored us. Fish boiled and covered with butter, garlic pottage, and fresh bread made an excellent meal. Then to bed early as I had a busy day.

I woke up to pee, but instead of reaching for the piss pot, I put on my robe and walked outside. The night was mostly clear, so I searched the sky as I stood there. Sure enough, I saw a visitor in the western sky, just above the tree line.

As I stood there considering this apparition, I heard the door to the house open, Astra joined me.

"So this is the star that the old man was telling you about," she said, "I've seen hairy stars before, usually lower on the horizon during the hour before dawn; this one looks different."

I could feel rather than see her stepping into her special place in her mind to view the night visitor. Only faint night sounds could be heard as she stiffened and stopped breathing. For what seemed a long time, but was probably only moments, I heard nothing. Then came the welcome heaving sound of her chest as she resumed breathing.

"The moon has washed out much of the color. Once the moon has set, it will be clearer. There is red, but other subtle colors as well. It's a warning. There is no doubt of it, but we must also look for other signs. Let us go inside; it is damp out here." We returned to our bed at this, but the old man had been right about the star, which I half thought resulted from his drunkenness.

The next morning, I was cleaning my workshop when I heard a horn in the distance, three shrill blasts, then answering calls closer. As I walked into the living area, I could sense the house springing to life. The alarm had transformed a tranquil home into a veritable hive of activity. A servant brought me my helmet and breastplate as I took my sword and shield from where they hung by the door. Within minutes horses were being hitched to the two wagons we owned as clothing, food, and cooking utensils were being gathered. Astra called out orders as the household prepared to flee for their lives. After everything had been loaded and checked, they would head for the quarry, where they would wait for word to either return or go south. I gave Astra some last-minute instructions as she fussed over the leather straps on my armor that I could never get tight enough. After hurried kisses to the children and suitable admonishments for them to mind their mother, I made for the door. As I strode forward in my martial habiliments, my mount was ready for me. I suspect that I looked more formidable than I felt. Still, I must play my part and stifle whatever doubts I might have. The little troop that would now follow me out of the gate needed all the encouragement and bravery that could be summoned; only one of them, old Thor, Nel's son, had ever done any fighting. He rode at my side similarly armed, except that his large frame was encased in a mail shirt instead of a breastplate. He was born somewhere in Scandia, fought for the Danes, fought against the Danes, and after taking an arrow through his left hand, he decided to take up farming. On foot, there were seven men with shields and spears. Behind them came four boys with slings. I waited until they had all cleared the gate, then stopped and took out my knife and made a small cut on my thumb, and smeared the blood on both the door and the post. Then I closed my eyes and said the words. The last person leaving would close the door, which would remain closed until I returned. Fire could not burn it, nor axes chop it until I removed the spell.

The strength of the village and its surrounding area was about 100 men and boys armed with swords, spears, scythes, flails, slings, and clubs studded with nails; hardly any had armor. A few more could be counted on from the more remote farms, but that would take time. As we approached the rally point on a small hill on the north side of the village overlooking the harbor, it looked to me like just about everyone had come. Men called out and waved to us as we rode closer; the mood was good; these were solid people, not easily spooked, at least in daylight.

Thor and I got off our horses, handing the reins to a youth with a pocked face and a long knife in his belt. Walking quickly to the front of the throng, I found the village elders standing in a group, obviously waiting for me."There's a ship out there coming this way. They'd been here already, but the winds shifted against them. They're rowing; she's a deep hull ship, no coaster, with a big mast; she had blood red sails plain as the hammer before she furled them."

"Red sails, you say?" wondered Thor as he fingered his scraggly blonde-grey beard that was his battleground for lice. "That can't be good." Everyone now looked at me because I was considered the repository of lore, facts, and gossip.

"The only people I have ever heard of with red sails would be the people of the Smoke Islands," I said after a few moments of thought, "but they aren't known as raiders; in fact, they aren't known for leaving their lands."

"You're right," said Thor, "I've heard of them. They're good ones to stay away from. They have islands," he said as he waved his hand to the northeast. "They are near Geats but not part of them. So they say, I've not seen them myself."

As they inched closer, I began to doubt their hostile intent. It was too far to see clearly, but we'd see the glint of the weapons and armor by now if these were raiders. Nor were the oars fully manned as they would have been if violence was in the offing. I counted only five on each side, just enough to keep it going in a wind like this.

"Well, boys, she looks like no raider to me. Let's all relax here while Thor and I talk to them. And you, one-eye," I said, calling out to a man on the other side of the hill, "you better come too; you speak Frisian. By the hammer, I don't know what talk these people use. Everyone else, stay here but don't wander; I want them to see you. It never hurts to let strangers know we are ready when we have to be." We had six languages between the three of us, which I thought would probably suffice.

As it turned out, they spoke the trade language of the Danes, which is easily understood. When they came close enough, a man in the bow made the universal sign of peace and greeting, a raised arm with an open palm. There were fourteen men altogether, no weapons, at least in the open. For clothing, they were dressed much the same as one would see anywhere on the coast. The only thing that seemed odd was that they were all very hairy with big black beards, bushy eyebrows, hairy arms and legs, and long hair, mostly braided. Yet the men differed in other ways, some being lean and some stout, some tall, some not, but none with brown or blond hair or red. All had the darkest hair and eyes I'd ever seen and a strange smell that I couldn't place. The reason for their visit was soon expressed when their leader asked to meet the "eater of magic who carves stones of enchantment." In other words, they came to see me.

The news that there would be no battle didn't disappoint anyone. They took it as a sign that they had worked too hard and needed the rest of the day off from toil. Most headed home with their weapons slung over their shoulders. A few stayed nearby when skins of wine were passed around. For myself, I had business to conduct. I sent Thor back to find the family and tell them what had transpired. Then I climbed aboard the ship to parley with the Smoke Islanders.

This took a great deal of time due to the inadequacy of the language to describe what they wanted. Their chief priest had died, and they wanted a memorial but not the usual kind. All their people were cremated except this one man, who was to be buried in a grave with offerings inside a large mound.

Then I remembered talking to a scribe in the service of a warlord in Rus, the same one my father worked for. He told me a tale of some dark and malevolent islands that were to be found somewhere east and north of the Danes. These people suffered no visitors; those who stopped innocently for water or washed up on their shores by a storm found themselves enslaved, except those who ended up as sacrifices to whatever Gods they served. They also coated themselves with repellent oils to keep wicked imps and dwarfs with sinus trouble away. Cruel Gods were not unheard of, yet the way their high priest was selected was very odd. Only a runaway slave who had killed his master, or a coward who fled a battle, was eligible to be a candidate. But before he could do that, he had to first take mistletoe from a tree in their sacred grove. If he was successful and many were slain in the attempt, he could challenge the existing high priest to combat and, if he won, would take over as the new priest. He would then rule the sacred shrine until he, in turn, was slain. This recollection helped me understand what they were trying to tell me.

It appeared that the recently deceased priest, who had served for many years, was now being kept on ice. They said he was skilled but so evil that they wanted to commemorate his life with a stone with strong spells to keep him from leaving his grave. Also, to keep his enemies, which he had many, from desecrating his grave.

Then I heard them say a sinister word I was quite familiar with *Necromantia*. Now more of what they said made sense. They were worried that somebody would raise their priest for some dark and unholy reason if such a thing were possible.

All people who have long winters like ours have heard tales of Necromancers. They are magicians who claim to raise the dead to learn information to their advantage or to haunt some unlucky soul. Some of the more frightening stories have the dead murdering the living in their sleep by hideous methods, including biting off an arm or squeezing a head until it popped like a grape. I heard my share of these stories when I was young; like most small boys, I loved to be scared with a good story.

As to more practical matters, they gave me a down payment of twenty silver coins, all were of good quality, but none were familiar. The variety and apparent age of some made me feel uncomfortable that I was being paid in the coin of the murdered. Perhaps I did them wrong to think such a thing; maybe. When the work was done, I knew there would be more; I was shown a fine gold bracelet decorated with green, red, and yellow stones that would be mine. Seeing it made my mouth water to see the look on Astra's face as I put it on her wrist.

A deal was struck, so I left the Islanders on their ship, and glad I was to go. Being near these people was no kindness to my nose. Many of them had a shine to their beard, butter? There was a puzzling smell that I later figured out: rancid butter. Was there meaning to this?

I would come again in a couple of days to settle on details and bring some drawings for them, also a draft of the wording. But first, I would have to find the right stone. This wasn't easy to do when dealing with a large memorial not done on the actual site. A stone would have to be selected, removed from the stone bed using only the most primitive tools, and taken back to my workshop, all at night. It was important that the stone never be exposed to sunlight, or the magic would fail. The stone would have to be without cracks or other faults; if it broke during shipping, it would be of no use to anyone, and my reputation, if not my throat, would suffer. I added up the probable days needed to finish this stone and found five; if all went well, it could be shipped on the sixth. If the weather was fair and my skill and luck were not failing me.

Late the following night, we had a reresupper in preparation for our foray into the quarry in search of a stone. This would take all the adult men in the household and a couple of hangers-on who would, for once, have to work in return for their meal. Prying a stone loose once a suitable one had been found, using only wooden wedges and mallets would be tricky. There was no sense in going out early, for, without moonlight, we'd have to rely solely on lanterns or torches. And when the moon rose above the horizon, we sallied forth with many a belch. There was a total of eleven of us. Old Thor and I were on horse, two in the wagon with the rest on foot. When we reached the quarry, the moon was up sufficiently to enable us to work. And work we did with various and sundry curses and appeals to the Gods as feet were trod on, and mallets found targets of flesh instead of flint wedges. Thor believed that if we removed the broken rock from the area where we had taken other stones, we could probably find something to work with if we could pull it out without breaking it. That was always the problem; one crack could turn a worthwhile stone fit to record the lives of heroes into a pile of worthless rubble as a testimony to the efforts of bumblers. But we were in luck; this bed of stone was clearly defined and about four fingers thick.

This took hours of work using only picks made of flint or deer horn and mallets of wood, and the most common tool of all, our hands. During periods of breath-catching, we paused to view the hairy star, which was in full view and heard the various explanations, some fanciful, others idiotic, as to what this strange visitor portended. The weather was tolerable but damp enough to provoke coughs and shivers.

Once the face of the stone was clean, I went to work. First, I took the chalk and, with a measuring square and stick, traced the rough outline. Then I took a special flint chisel and held it to the rock, following the lines as Thor rapped it with the wooden mallet. This wasn't easy, but we moved along quickly once we got into a rhythm. We went back and forth, up and down, scoring and chipping it as well as we could. We didn't worry about the underside; previous experience showed that the stone would easily separate along the seam it laid on.

At last, the moment of truth arrived; it was the first of several critical tests that must be passed. First, we would have to separate the stone along its long axis. And if successful, the top and bottom would be attempted. This called for brute strength and luck. None of my spells had ever made the removal of stone any easier, unfortunately. I put a special flint chisel in the groove of the stone we had just cut and held it there as steady as I could while Thor hit it with a solid blow, then another. It took three hard hits to make the first break; it followed the scored line for a good arm's length before stopping. This we repeated, with success, until the cracked outline of the stone had been established; by this time, we were both covered in sweat and dust. But there was no rest; time was getting on.

Removing the stone was not child's play; when stood on end, it would reach my chin and be nearly as wide as my shoulders, a good four fingers thick, and of course, heavy.

The appeals to the Gods must have helped, for we got the stone securely lashed to a wooden frame and covered with hides just as the first faint rays of the sun appeared in the east. With the stone safely stowed in the wagon, we turned towards home, the horses straining in the harness from the weight and our hands straining to reach the skins of wine now being passed around.

The morning of the following day, I journeyed through the village to the harbor where my clients were waiting aboard their ship. There was a fair amount of activity on the beach as a coastal trading vessel was offering all sorts of wares for sale or trade. This was important to the locals because, in winter, several families engaged in the manufacture of high-quality bows and arrows. There was also cloth for sale and iron to buy. At the moment, a spirited debate was taking place over the exchange of arrows for barrels; unfortunately, there was no local cooper.

The Smoke Islanders had pulled their ship far enough on the beach for me to board easily by swinging myself over the side. After exchanging the usual salutes of greeting, a horn of some dubious alcoholic brew was thrust into my hand. I was able to swallow a small swig of this concoction and smile at the same time, quite a feat considering just how vile it tasted.

After being seated on the bench of an oar, the three chief men began to talk with me about the particulars of their commission. I described the stone and the fact that it was large enough for just about any reasonable number of inscriptions and drawings and, of course, enchantments.

"How close to a dwelling is the burying ground that he will lie in?" I was informed that the island burial ground was remote and a part of the island nobody lived or often visited.

"Perfect," I replied, "then nobody will be hurt by the pillar of flame that will reach into the sky if his burial stone is disturbed after it's put in place." While this was not strictly true, it didn't do any harm to inflate my abilities. In the long run, it might make people less likely to put my powers to the test.

Once the real purpose of this memorial stone was revealed, all the details fell into place. I made them an offer of hospitality, at least as far as a meal went, but they were not very interested. Perhaps they viewed our cooking as unappetizing. More likely, they were not used to being away from home, and their insular society made them overly suspicious of others. The odor of rancid butter, which I had noted before, still made my nose tingle. Nobody else could understand why these people should anoint themselves with such a scent; it remained as one of those minor unresolved mysteries that happen in life. Perhaps in my old age, I could remember to look for an answer.

That night I sat with Astra in my workshop as I prepared to work on the stone, which was now resting on the floor, being far too heavy for my workbench. I shared a cup of wine with her as I considered the project, nervously fingering a piece of white chalk in my hand. Once I started, there would be no conversation and very little reasoning ability within me once the rune magic began. But I hung back, talking to Astra before taking the plunge.

"So these hairy visitors who bring you gold and silver are afraid of their old priest returning to haunt them?" She asked as she looked over my tools, careful not to touch any.

"A ghost will usually only haunt one specific place or person. But yes, that does worry them. As a living man, he was evil enough; as a shade or a ghost, he could be much worse. But if there is an outside force at work, a Necromancer, for instance, could use that dead priest to terrible effect. That is something to be truly fearful of." As I said this, I felt the hair on the back of my neck rise, for even the thought of such a creature was frightening.

"Such creatures," I said, looking her in the eye, "are filled with rage and hatred toward the living. They hate everything about us, our breath, heartbeat, and warmth. They are only interested in destruction and, once animated, can't be easily controlled or extinguished."

"So, what about those who inhabit the barrows and grave mounds? One hears many stories of them; unwary travelers being abducted underground, never to be seen again."

"I asked my father about that, and he advised me never to walk near such places if I could help it. Only in the noonday sun is one safe, which is why burials always take place at that time of day. There are also those who were slain in these places to stand a ghostly guard over a treasure or grave goods."

"Is it possible to converse with such creatures?"

She asked. "Perhaps," I replied after some thought. "But if you weren't very careful, it could easily be the last conversation you will ever have. Being whisked away to the cold and damp home of an evil spirit is not a pleasant thought; I hope you don't dream of such things."

"You never really said how you were told about the runes," Astra said, changing the topic away from cold graves and hauntings. "Your father seldom mentioned it, yet he carved hundreds of stones. He was even more silent on the subject than you are. And when I think of it, I confess I don't know much about them except for what little you tell me. But tell me first, before it slips my mind, are these people you now work for connected to the swart dwarfs? Sometimes dwarfs are mentioned in stories; they sound similar to these people." She said as she stooped down to inspect the stone as it lay there on its wooden cradle, raw and uncovered.

"You are full of questions tonight; I'm surprised you've heard of the Swart dwarfs. They are not a very common subject for conversation and not very common to find either; thank the Gods for that. They are sullen, unhappy creatures that are known for their greed besides their bad tempers. They have magic, certainly, but they were cursed by the fates and the All-Father with bad luck. While they are constantly scheming and plotting, few of their endeavors are successful. Still, they are reputed to be wondrous goldsmiths, and it can't be denied that they furnished the Gods with some wondrous weapons and tools. As to your question about runes, I can only tell you what he said; I recall it well enough." Here I took the bronze flagon and poured some wine into my cup. "I don't think I was past my tenth year when he told me the lore of the runes. For a man who was often silent, he could tell a rare, good tale when he had to." Then taking a seat on a stool across from where she stood, I repeated what my father had told me many years earlier.

"At the center of all creation is the great tree Yggdrasil. It upholds the heavens and binds the world together with its roots. At the base of the tree is Asgard, the home and fortress of the Gods of whom Woden, whom the Danes and those who live in Scandia call Odin.

"This sacred tree grows from the Well of Urd, a fathomless pit that contains the most potent magical forces in creation. But the well was guarded by the giant Mirir, who allowed none to drink from its waters. When Odin craved a drink of it, the giant couldn't outright refuse him because he was a God but instead leveled a heavy toll, an eye, as payment for a horn full of the magical water. Odin agreed to this, and the giant gouged out an eye. After this, the giant was compelled to let him drink the water of knowledge.

"After drinking from the magical pool, Odin perceived many things that were heretofore hidden. He found that this pool is tended by the Norns, three wise maidens who are the fates who control all destinies in the Nine Worlds. He saw the maidens shape their will by carving wooden slates with letters called runes. Odin envied the wise maidens and put his mind to learning the secret of this writing.

"The runes only reveal themselves to those worthy and able to withstand the sight of such fearful abilities and power. As in all things, like the horn of wisdom Odin gave an eye for, payment was required. That's why Odin pierced himself with a spear that pinned him to the sacred tree. After nine days, he died, but since he was immortal, he returned to life. Then he saw the runes appear close to him, so he snatched them with his hands.

"The runes could carry magic; this added to his formidable powers. With them, he could overcome practitioners of malevolent magic and the dead that served them. Neither could their spells bind him or those whom he wished to protect. His penetrating and agile mind was made sharper, and his healing powers greatly improved.

"But Odin has never been the God of the ordinary man. No, he has always been the God of princes, warlords, and those of power. Yet, in one respect, this episode of the runes gave another class of men access to his ear. He was the God of those who were about to be hung. If the rope was in your near future, it was to Woden that you appealed to."

"So, the power of the runes comes from the magical well," she said after a moment of reflection.

"That's only part of it; the well that holds that magic overflows into our world, Midguard, where it streams like an underground river throughout the world. Nobody knows where this river of magic is located."

"But that never stopped anyone from guessing," she said, smiling.

"My grandfather made some guesses, some of which are recorded in those scrolls," I said, pointing to a shelf where rolled-up parchments could be seen.

"But as to your question," I continued, "runes can be much more than just symbols that make words. But if you want to make them your magical servants, you must be born with power and then be trained to use it, which is no easy task."

"Will you summon the power tonight? Will it be sufficient for your visitors who reek of old butter?"

"I hope so," I replied with a smile.

"Then to bed I go," she said, straightening, "I'd better see the children first. Try not to bring the house down upon our heads with your incantations and wine."

I sensed that calling up the magic for this stone would be challenging, so I called on Thor and my son Flosi for assistance. Thor had helped me before, but for Flosi, it would be his first. Witnessing the spells of rune power would be a lot for a boy of his age, but he was game for it and excited to be considered adult enough to take part.

Before I started, I composed my mind by chanting softly to myself, an incantation used by the runemasters who went before me. It would quicken my spirit and awaken the power within me for the task ahead. Each of the twenty-four runes had to be called by their names using the ancient poem:

Dagaz *tells Odin's tale,* ***Inwaz*** *holds a spear,* ***Yera*** *for fallen leaves,* ***Ansus*** *for times forgotten,* ***Raithto*** *is a white stallion,* ***Wunjo*** *summons power.*

As I finished these familiar words, I noted a red tinge in my sight, a sure sign that my abilities were now being brought to full power. Yet there were things to do before making the chips fly. Standing in front of the small workshop fireplace, I reached in among the twigs and shavings of wood with my mind summoning a spark to start the fire. Proof was needed that I was worthy to cut the runes of magic.

My grandfather could start a fire with a simple snap of his fingers. In fact, he would make the fire jump from finger to finger. That was beyond my abilities; my father's too. I felt a little moisture upon my brow before I smelled the first whiff of smoke; not my best effort, I thought. But my assistants saw nothing amiss; both were suitably impressed. From the look on their faces, I half expected to see them make the sign against enchantment which would not, of course, be very effective. The fire had the very mundane and welcomed effect of getting the dampness out of the room. Summer was still some weeks away, and the nights were still chilly. I knew that I would be sweating later, but the flames felt good for the moment as they danced in the hearth. I had one last thing to do before I started the repetitive chant that I would use while chipping; it was the *Black Drink*. I took a kettle of water from the fireplace as soon as it was hot and poured it into a large wooden cup. Into this, I poured a small amount of a foul-smelling herbal brew that I had recently ground and mixed. It should be at full potency tonight; my first sip told me I was correct in this estimation. This drink, so potent that it had a cult following among the Rus, helped me chant the Runes of Power as I worked. The words would become more difficult to say the longer I took to complete the spell. Without the drink, my mouth would feel like I had swallowed a tree trunk, and I wouldn't be able to articulate the words, which would, of course, make the spell fail. Now, with a nod to my assistants, I began. Thor had helped me before, but this was my son's first time seeing magic close up.

I used a flint chisel positioning it for each blow that Thor gave with the wooden hammer. Flosi's job was to whisk away the chips of stone with a brush: he also fetched me a drink of the herbal brew when I needed it. There was no conversation from this point on; I was fully in the grip of the runes. I had no idea of the exact letters I was carving, although I could see them in my mind's eye. Fire-like they flashed before me as I toiled. Beforehand I had carefully thought out what needed to be said; this was essential, of course, yet in the end, futile, for the spell decided for itself the wording.

What I wanted was a powerful and long-lasting spell to keep this person under the ground and unmolested. As to how that would be expressed, only the runes would know. Later I got the feeling that anyone who tried to raise this man as a ghost or reanimated body would find themselves as a permanent resident lodged beneath this stone, just as dead as the man it covered. While I can never know precisely how long the curse will last, as a practical matter, this priest would be dust before the curse dissipated; of that, I was pretty sure. It is known to savants, though, that there is a balance between the power of a curse and its longevity. As a rule, the stronger the curse, the shorter it would last.

An hour later, I was done with the cutting and ready to rest, and we all needed to piss. So, we stumbled out the workshop door and relieved ourselves in the nearby bushes. It was good that there was nobody to see us, for we'd have scared them covered as we were with dust; indeed, we looked more like ghosts than live beings. Wordlessly we returned inside, where I took the last sip of the Black Drink, tossing the dregs into the fire, which caused it to flare.

Now I readied myself for the final and most challenging step in finishing the stone. I grabbed a bowl, pestle, and a sharp stone knife and sat at my bench. Then I took a small cup of goat's milk and mixed in ground red ocher, after which I started a low and melodious chant. As I mouthed the words, I took the knife and cut open a small vein on my wrist as I held it over the bowl.

The blood flowed into the bowl, but instead of slowing down as it would in a normal cut, it speeded up, much to the dismay of my son and Thor. Of course, I had heard of spell thirst but had never experienced it myself; there were stories of enchanters found dead from this, their bodies nothing but dry husks. I mentally damned the greed of this spell, but there was nothing I or anyone else could do; the bowl was now half full and showed no sign of slowing. I struggled to finish the chant, but I was almost overwhelmed by a buzzing in my ears like a giant bee too close for comfort. Then, just as I started panting, it stopped; a last drop of blood fell into the bowl, after which the cut disappeared as it had never been there at all.

Carefully I mixed the ingredients together in the bowl that was now filled almost to the rim, and even more carefully, I lowered it to the floor next to the stone. Then I took a brush made of pine marten bristles, dipped it into the mixture, and applied it to the runes. The stone absorbed nearly all of it, leaving only token amounts in the cuts. I was surprised that my arms had any strength left in them after the ordeal of the bleeding, but I kept up a brisk pace until I was finished. It was only then that I looked down and read the words that I had carved and bled for:

The oars are silent—the mast broke-- waves wash over the ship--souls of valiant men will not linger--the Gods will redeem their spirits--in far islands dead moan--shield wall broken—banners in dying wind—ravens on ravaged land-- no fell man bring life to the dead--rune spells protect --scatter bones of wicked spell casters--I Arn cut this stone.

Later after the work was done and my son and Thor were gone, I sat resting in my chair; I felt my sleepy mind drifting away; it seemed like I was out of my body, hovering like a bird floating in the wind. Then came a profound stillness followed by sudden warmth and the far-away cry of gulls.

I was sitting in the stern of a small dory with my grandfather Gudgaest Hammer-Hand at the oars. I was always happy to see him. For a young boy, everything about him was bigger than normal--the size of his shoulders, the fullness of his beard, and the boom of his voice.

"I see you've come for a history lesson, boy. Do you know when and where we are?"

"No, grandfather," I said as I looked about in what appeared to be an early morning haze. Patches of fog drifted eerily about; the sun seemed distant and cold. We were among some islands, but nothing was familiar to me.

"It's the third year of King Bjorn Bjornson the Old's reign in South Dane land. Look about, boy, and tell me what you see?"

"I see two fleets heading towards each other," I said as the fog began to blow away, "Will there be a battle?" I asked after taking a long hard look around me. Immediately I thought that I had asked a stupid question. Where there were opposing groups of ships, there was always a battle.

"A battle like no other, he replied with a laugh, but it was not between these two fleets. No, I was able to spare them that although Jarl Hakon Harefoot, over yonder," he said, pointing over my shoulder in the distance, "was willing enough to fight. But I wouldn't let him unless there was no other way because every man of his that was killed would become an enemy due to an evil enchantment. This was no ordinary fight; you are right to widen your eyes at this," he said with another laugh; I'm sure that your father told you some of this, but now it's time that you learn all. The world is always dangerous, so you need to know your enemy and have your wits about you.

"It all started with a man who called himself a Dane, Harald of Hedeby; he said as he pulled the oars in and got himself seated a bit more comfortably, although I doubt that he had ever been to Hedeby and his name probably wasn't even Harald. At other times he said that he was a younger son of a warlord in Scandia; another time, he said he was the bastard son of a Frisian nobleman. But he was such a fantastic liar that nothing he said could be believed."

"What we know for sure," he continued as he looked down at me, "is that when little more than a boy, he joined a Frankish order of Christian monks down in Thuringia. According to what was learned later, he noted that during a time of famine, the monks were the last to go hungry. In this, he was right, of course. After all," grandfather said with a snort, "how can a God be served if his servants are all dead?"

"Be that as it may, he showed an early ability in reading and writing. Also in languages, even ones no longer spoken. This fact brought him to the notice of their leaders, and he would have probably risen high in their church had it not been for his drunkenness, lechery, and thefts. Another man would have been thrown out the door with many kicks and blows, but he was far too useful to be let go. They sent him to a remote abbey in the south to translate some documents discovered in an old fortress of the Roman people, a mighty race who once ruled the world. He was given a collection of scrolls that the Romans had taken from some evil priests in Gaul, far to the west. These priests ruled a vast and wealthy region that were related somehow to the Celts we often hear of. The Romans were a warrior people not easily impressed by death and destruction, yet they viewed those priests, whose names we do not know, with great horror for their ingenuity in human sacrifice. One of their vile methods of honoring their Gods was constructing great cages out of sticks and the wands of willow trees. They were many feet high and built in the shape of men or animals; inside these cages, they herded their wretched sacrifices. Then they piled wood around the bottom and set it on fire roasting the people inside alive. One must ask, what sort of Gods would enjoy the sweet music of people being burned alive? As bad as this was, they invented even crueler means of torment. They would bury them alive and then dig them up the following day, after which, by use of divers and bestial arts of dark magic, they were brought back to life. Not a full life, of course, only a corrupted shade's existence of slavery, pain, sorrow, and an all-consuming rage. When the Romans found these horrible creatures, they recoiled in horror and killed every priest they could lay their hands on. This would have been the end of it except some Roman, not understanding the full nature of these savage priests, took as many of their books as he could find at sent them back to the great Roman fortress, I mentioned, which in time became the abbey where this unruly monk was sent.

"At some point, his depraved nature must have gotten him into trouble again, for we know that he killed the Abbot, stole the abbey's money and silver altar pieces, and headed north. For several years we heard little of him except for a report that he had taken a ship and turned pirate. But then he turned up again, this time among the coastal Cours, as an adviser to one of the petty kings that infested that region.

"Here, he gained some prominence as a man of magic and a seer. It was said that he could talk to the dead to learn where treasure was buried and, by other dark and unknown methods, learn the fates of men. He was widely sought after in the matter of omens and divination. He grew fantastically rich, so much so that the man he served, Osric the Younger, resolved to kill him. But the priest struck first and poisoned his drink one night. On the third day after his death, he raised Osric, or what was left of him, and paraded him around in chains as a symbol of his magical power, which was, at this point, considerable.

"He now covered his shaved priest's pate with a crown of gold and precious stones and covered himself with costly royal clothing. With all restraint gone, he held unholy revels where he gorged himself on his grotesque and ludicrous perversions. All were terrified of him, and those unfortunate to live close to his lands made haste to give him whatever they had in the way of coin or animals. This went on for some years as his reputation spread far and wide.

Here grandfather paused for a snort of derision and laughter that seemed very much out of place considering the subject he was describing."As a ruler, he was as bad a demon as the nine worlds could produce. But he did manage to find a cure for the pains of old age," he said with a snigger, "when a man lived to be too old to work, he simply slit his throat!" Here he removed a square of cloth from up his sleeve and wiped his eyes as he fought down further laughter. At length, he composed himself and continued his story.

"But in the world we live in, there is no curse worse that having a reputation for wealth. As soon as it was known that this monk turned King was rich, greedy men began to covet his wealth. Hard men who lived as soldiers and spent little time out of the leather harness of war looked at his kingdom coolly appraising the odds. The threats came from both near and far.

"This was known to the monk who by now had taken the name of King of the Cours--but most called him *The King of Death*. He learned their intentions quickly, for as depraved as he was, he was careful enough to have spies among those who had the ability to do him the most harm. He was in a fix; in the spring, a fleet of ships would be outside his harbor; his own ships were few, and his army small. Others in his situation would have hurried to hire mercenaries, of which there was always plenty. But he knew, from greater wisdom than he had a right to, that mercenaries fight for pay. They were not bold fighters; the mighty deeds that they were famous for were performed at the table and involved food and drink. There were simply none at hand who would fight for him out of either love or duty. So, what to do? It is said that while torturing a wandering Christian missionary who had fallen into his clutches, he began to devise a plan."

"Grandfather, how did you become involved with all this? And why did he take such a stupid-sounding name for his title instead of the mighty or the fearsome? I asked. And what is this place called that we are in?"

"You ask many questions, young one; that's the problem with questions; they require answers. But I suppose that you deserve a few. First," he said, moving his hand in a broad circle, "we are in what was once The Bay of Gulls just off the coast of the Cours. After the battle, that was not really a battle in the accepted sense; it's been known as *The Bay of Corpses*. As to the names of kings, such titles as The Bold, The Mighty, or The Wise are usually given after the ruler is dead and found to be deserving of such an honor. Names given in life are usually less heroic such as Olaf the Stout or Guthrum the Lame. As for my own involvement, it is quite simple. I was at the court of King Bjornson the Old and did as much as I could to promote this venture. I considered it only a matter of time before that bloated hound of destruction would become bored and seek conquest, and it would be better to exterminate him before he got any more powerful. What was I doing in his court, you ask? I was earning my bread as a master of runes because the king was shrewd enough to know I was more than a simple stone-chipper.

"I warned King Bjornson that raiders and petty kings were preparing to attack the mad ruler of the Cours, but they wouldn't succeed. If anything, they would just add to the number of corpses he was said to control. I urged him to attack immediately in order to wipe out this blight before it spread. He agreed with me, but I know he suspected the necromancer was wealthy, which made the attack more enticing.

"We set sail so early in the season that ice could still be seen on the fringe of the fjord as we sailed out all those years ago; we had a hundred ships packed with the best manhood of the land led by the youthful Jarl Hakon Harefoot, the king's right hand in matters of battle. We knew naught what to expect; even those who took omens were confused. Those who took wine instead of prophecy were better off; for me, I put my faith in the All-Father and the fates which bound me to him.

"As we entered this bay, we saw, and smelled, the ships opposed to us. Their so-called King had bought many ships from Scandia and elsewhere. The variety of these vessels earned hoots from our men when they came into view. There was all manner of coastal barges, ships of war, ships of trade, fishing boats, and the like. Some old, some new, all with decks full of what looked like warriors."

"But grandfather," I cried out, interrupting his talk, "how can we see the past? Are we dead? I am a boy here, yet I am not a boy. Is this just happening in my head? Is this real, or is it just a wild vision?"

"Of course, this is a vision," laughed the old man, "yet it is real enough. Yes, it's in your head, but you're not dead in the least. The spell you worked on is one of real power, by far the most potent you've ever produced, yet you will need to do far better in the times ahead. The wolf comes," he said, putting a finger next to his nose. "Many will depend on you; now, let me finish this tale."

"The mad monk-king gathered all the people of his largest island and told them that he had stolen a great secret from the Christians while he was a monk. By now, the entire world had heard of their strange rite where they symbolically eat the flesh and drink the blood of their executed God. The ordinary people had an imperfect understanding of this, so they believed him when he said he could give them eternal life by using the secret, yet harmless, rite that the priests selfishly kept for themselves. Had they not seen his great feats of magic? Perhaps this one time, he might put his powers to something beneficial. After all, they reasoned, what was mere gold and silver compared to life itself? Eternal life at that. He did no such thing, of course; he betrayed every last one of them. He had a great table covered with silk cloth set up in the middle of town. Here he sat, and with his own hands, he poured out cups of wine that he claimed were part of the Christian ceremony. He made a great show of piety by wearing only his monk's robe with a large cross hung around his neck on a chain. He blessed every person who came forward to claim their drink. The spiced wine was indeed good; it contained the milk of squeezed poppies and other herbs that dulled the mind. When all had drunk, he bade them come forward to enjoy a feast of the Christ God which, he said, was only boar flesh and goose livers. By the following day, they would all know and feel the great power that he had so generously shared with them. In this, he told the truth, for by the next morning, all of them felt his power, but not in the manner that they wished for.

"As they stood in line, most took trenchers made of flatbread that was provided. Only a few took the unfamiliar wooden dishes that were coming into fashion. Upon bread or wood, the minions of the mad king piled slices of what they were told were savory meat and fowl. But what they got were slices of rotted livers, kidneys, and brains cut from the bodies of dead men. The wine fuddled the wits and hid the putrid taste and smell of the offal they consumed. That night those who attended this feast of decay died a most horrible death. Imagination averts its eyes at the suffering they must have endured, and one can only imagine the stench of the vomit and excrement they were covered in.

"The next day, the king of this scene of death continued his blasphemy against nature when he rose them up from the dead. There they stood on the shore, ravers straining to be let loose against the living. They had no weapons; they needed none. To look upon them was terror itself. More than that, they had teeth to bite and inhuman strength to rend. Only decapitation was a sure way to bring them down. And any that they bit or chewed on would very likely join their foul ranks. When word came of the approaching fleet, they were driven onto ships where they were put to the oars."

"But how could they row if they were dead, grandfather?" I blurted out, "but weren't you scared?"

"They didn't row very well, that is true. Yet the inhuman willpower of their master lashed them on. But in truth, our men didn't row so well either once they got a good look at who they were expected to fight. As to being scared, he paused to finger his beard, that is difficult to say. All that day, I had felt a power or a strength rising within me. Yet I must say that when we saw the pus-filled eyes and dripping ears of the undead coming towards us, I felt as sick as any man on the ship." Here he paused for a moment, obviously filled with emotion at the remembrance of that day.

"You have to remember that when the earth power that we call magic is used to create death and destruction, it will provoke a reaction. That is what happened that day; I felt my spirit and inner magical strength rising like never before. And my years of struggle, and with failure too, had toughened me and made my hide like that of a walrus," he said with a laugh. "This so-called King of the Islands who wielded this blood magic was in for a sore surprise. You see, my young friend, as I said, I felt the power rising within me as we came upon the fleet of the dead. I also admit to a degree of vanity as I must have cut a very fine figure dressed as I was in my black leather jerkin with the bosses and shoulder guards of polished brass. My helm was the finest in all the ships; I made it, you know, myself. Here he paused to sit sideways on the boat seat as we watched the ships in the distance. I also made a shield and painted it many runes of protection. As we neared the death ships, I stood in the bow of the lead ship with Jarl Hakon Harefoot, who must have thought me mad. With one hand on the throat of the carved dragon on the bow and the other holding a war axe, I ordered the men to change course, for I had spied the ship that carried their foul king. It was a warship very much like ours, only painted blood red. Her decks were crewed with the scum who served him, who beat their swords and axes against their shields as we approached, making a hellish din. Soon we were on them; we wove our way through their line like a snake swimming through a bunch of ducks and planted our ship along his with hooks and lines. The action was lively as arrows flew and spears were thrown. Over the side we went with a shout and a clash of arms. I used my shield edge to knock one man into the water while the others fled before my swinging axe. I saw this so-called king in the stern, holding a club as he directed his forces. His face was as ugly as any in the nine worlds; he looked like a large and belligerent frog." The old man said as he paused for a hearty laugh, "he wasn't happy to see me, I can tell you that. He spat curses at me and raised his spiked club to strike me, but I caught it on my shield. The blow exploded with a deafening sound and drove me to my knees. But I was soon on my feet again, though," he said laughing, "in those days, I was much leaner! At any road, the fight was soon over. I jumped to my feet, and before he could do more, I split the crown of his head open with my axe. So ended the reign of the Death King.

"Things fell apart very quickly then. The reanimated dead returned to their natural state as their ships, now without any guidance, smashed into the rocks dumping their bodies into the bay known thereafter as the *Bay of Corpses*.

"None of this madman's servants, the ones alive that is, survived of course. They were soon stripped, and their bodies were thrown into the bay to join the others. Later that day, Hakon Harefoot and I went ashore and visited the headquarters of the fallen lunatic. We were able to set free a few poor souls who had been languishing in his cells, presumably awaiting torment of some kind. From what we were told, his retainers vied with each other in inventing cruel tortures for his wretched victims.

"I found his quarters and his private library but, much to my disgust, I was too late. His papers and scrolls had already been ransacked. Clearly, somebody wanted to learn his secrets and wasted no time doing so. After examining what was left, I had the whole building burned to the ground.

"We stayed on the island only one night as we were anxious to return home to celebrate our victory. The men were very pleased when we found great amounts of treasure hidden near his dungeon."

"You were quite a warrior," I said in admiration, "my father never told me the details of how you won the day against that mad king. The world is better off without him, I think."

"Yes, indeed, we are better off, but there is more. And it concerns you." Here he bit his lip and turned to me, "as we were leaving, a boy came to me and told me something of grave import. He had been a serving lad in the kitchens and knew everyone in the king's retinue. He says that a man named Hundar kept records and was far into his lord's confidence. He was ill-favored, dark, short, and wholly evil, but also inquisitive, quick, and intelligent. It was said that he was a northern Wend, but that is not certain. The boy saw him leave with a sack full of his master's books and scrolls. This worried me greatly, for I now understood somewhat of his master's history. It was a bitter thought that such evil might again be unleashed upon the world.

"When we returned home, I got King Bjornson to send messages out in all directions offering ten marks of pure gold for the head of this Hundar, but nobody ever collected it. I went to the order of monks he once belonged to and learned what I could. I even went to the old Roman fortress in Thuringia, where the kindly abbot listened in horror to my story and then told me what he could about the maniacal monk who once lived in their abbey.

"But I never heard more until recently. The news comes from Scandia of the most unsettling kind. Fell things happen which remind me all too much of the insane king that was defeated years ago. You wonder how I can know these things even though I am gone from you, he said, seeing a question beginning to form on my lips, but even in the beyond, one hears things. So, I came to warn you. Perhaps this death king found a way to return, or maybe his former servant has put to use the information contained in the books that he stole."

"But why me? What can I do?" I blurted out.

"That is the question we all ask and never get an answer to. But now listen to me, boy, for my time here grows short. You have great abilities, and with that ability comes great responsibility. You cannot lie fallow in luxury and idleness far from the great problems of our times. Nor can you hide so far up the arse of the world that nobody can find you. That goes for your wife too. She has magic but lacks instruction; teach her the discipline of power, for she will be called upon to do great things. Pray to the Gods once in a while, not too often though, as they are busy, and trust in yourself and your wife, and study the words that your father left you. But now I must return, my beloved grandson. Perhaps we will meet again."

"Grandfather . . ." I tried to call, but the words caught in my throat.

"He turned to me again, smiled, took the oars in hand, and began rowing. I looked down at my feet and found I was now standing on a sandy beach. Then the vision began to dissolve into a mist of white and blue; in the distance, I heard the call of gulls."

The next day I inspected my work. Everything looked in order; the runes were cut neatly and stained with the mixture that contained my essence. But as I stared at it, I wondered about the magic; I couldn't really tell how effective it would be. My father confessed to me once that he would question his work but that it was a waste of time; either the magic worked, or it didn't.

We packed the stone in rowan leaves and wrapped it in tarps before returning it to the wooden frame on which it came from the quarry. Later we took it through the village down to the harbor; as usual, we were followed by a group of small boys trailing behind us. Word had gotten out that I had plied my trade again; the villagers liked it; when I prospered as I was liberal with feasting.

With much heaving and grunting, it was put on board and payment made. I suspect they had been talking to the locals, who were always happy to dwell on my abilities when talking to strangers. They must have felt a little intimidated because besides giving me the coins and gold bracelet, they included two big coils of ship cables made from walrus hide. Such things were always in demand and easy to sell or trade.

As I shared a final cup of wine with them as they waited for the land breeze, I asked them about the goings on in Scandia that they had mentioned. They said little, but it took no magic to see the look on their faces when I brought the subject up. This played on my mind in the following days. The following week I took a borrowed sailboat out an hour's sail into the sea with Astra. There she used her mind to influence the wind's direction and raise it. This was exceedingly difficult for her at first, and there was much failure. So, I shared with her a mental training discipline I had learned years ago. My father called it the *training of the three birds*. This involved trying to see things from a great height like a hawk, then at night like an owl, and then down through water like an egret. This method is hard to explain; many mental exercises are like that, yet she made progress.

After this, we made sailing a regular part of our lives. By degrees, she improved; at mid-summer, she could bring forth a squall from out of a calm day which sometimes put my sailing abilities to the test. There was much mirth and good cheer as we sailed about, always within sight of the land, of course, for the sea was infested with raiders. In later years, we looked back on this as a very happy period of our lives.

Chapter Two
To the King's Court

That autumn, in the month of Haustmanour for the Danes (for the rest of us, it was the month of the sow), everyone, including myself, was concerned with getting in the harvest. With the weather fair, there are no slackers. This bountiful harvest greatly improved the mood of the locals, who knew that this winter, no matter what the weather, enough food would be found for all. There would be an excess to sell too. Traders were always happy to take payment for goods in grain, for the Danes could never grow enough wheat to satisfy the demand.

But the promise of a full belly didn't alleviate the underlying unease I had felt growing ever since the visit of the Smoke Islanders. One thing that put a damper on the happy mood of the villagers was the hairy star that continued slowly growing in brightness and developing a tail. This, along with other omens such as the birth of a two-headed calf and the reported sighting of a bestial man-like creature with big feet, caused some clucking of tongues and wags of the head. Also, to be fair, some laughter among the more skeptical. But spurious reports notwithstanding, almost everyone thought something unsavory was happening in their world. I noticed a marked increase in the number of sacrifices to the Gods.

When a man wishes to offer a sacrifice, he will take the freshly killed animal and hang it from a pole outside his door before cooking it, so his neighbors will know that he offers meat to the Gods. The Gods, being Gods, have no actual use for the roasted animals, so everyone joins in on the feast. Over the summer, I saw pigs, goats, fowl, and sheep hanging in front of doors. Besides increased sacrifices, another sign of concern was the resurrection of the oft-debated plan to enclose the village in defenses. This time it was more than just idle talk. Piracy was on the increase; their boldness was shocking. Traders told tales of rapine and slaughter of helpless villages very much like our own, and harrying an enemy's coast was a tried-and-true tactic of war everywhere. No vote needed to be taken since everyone favored building a stout wall guarded by a ditch. I had some ideas about what should be done since I had seen many fortified places in my travels, and for that reason, I was given the task of designing the fortifications.

The night of the first frost found me sitting in the corner of our bedroom next to the fireplace, calculating the material and manpower requirements for the defense project. We would need 700 pines for the perimeter, including the roofed-over archer platform on the corner tops. Two small towers to flank the main entrance and the drawbridge and gate with corner posts would require another 100 trees, perhaps oak. The trees would have to be large enough to withstand the effects of fire arrows but remain small enough to be moved by teams of oxen. The trees would need to be marked and felled soon, for this work would need to be done in the winter so that they could be dragged in the snow for easier transportation. I estimated that with the available manpower, it could be done in three years, the first year for felling the trees, removing all the branches and bark, cutting them to length, and sharpening the tops. Then, in warmer weather, we would dig the trenches and lower the logs into position, after which we could build the gate, the drawbridge, and the rest of the fortifications. Then a ditch deep enough to hinder attackers would have to be dug. Of course, numerous other things would need to be done and problems of all sorts to deal with, but yes, it could be finished in three years, two if we felt the need for haste.

I put down my quill and scrap of parchment on the small table next to me and leaned back on the pine bench against the wall. The fire and a cup of mulled wine made me very comfortable. Soon my mind began to drift away from my previous images of men felling trees and digging ditches.

I was seated in the front of a wagon full of hay with the reins in my hands as I bumped along a rutted country road. The weather was sunny, warm, and bright, with just enough breeze to keep the flies away. The dark grey horses pulling the wagon were the short and stocky breed so often seen on the fringes of the Salt Sea. Just then, one of the horses nickered, making me aware of a figure in the near distance standing on the side of the road facing away from me. As we drew closer, I could see his grey hat with its low, bell-shaped crown and wide brim. His long robe belted in the middle was the same color; in his left hand, he held a long staff like a shepherd's crook. When I drew closer, I stopped the horses and looked down at him. As his face was still averted, I could see little except for his long grey hair and the fringe of his beard.

"Stranger," I said after a moment, "there is room next to me in the wagon if you would rather ride than walk."

"By the All-Father's missing eye, I am ready to sit." Here he turned towards me and, pulling a square of cloth from his robe, wiped his face. The blond-gray-streaked beard and the craggy visage sparked the light of recognition in me.

"Grandfather," I mumbled in disbelief, "what are you doing here? Wherever here is, of course." I said, looking around. "I think I'm lost, for that matter."

"No, you are not lost; you are HERE," he said with a laugh, pointing to the ground. "No matter where we are, it's good to see you, my boy!" At this, I made to jump down from the wagon, but he waved me back and walked around to the other side, where he hoisted himself up and onto the seat.

"Where are we going?" I asked as I shook the reins.

"I'm not going anywhere; this is where I live."

"I think where you live is inside my head. I seem to remember sitting by the fire working on plans for the village wall."

"You are still there, lad." Here he chortled as he put his big arm around my shoulders. "It's a worthy project. But it will take more effort than you think; things like this always do."

"So why am I delivering a load of hay?" I asked, "And to whom?"

"You are sleeping in your room with your wife in bed; this just represents your trip to Roskilde."

"So I am going to the capital of the Danes? Why should I do that? It's a long way off and the wrong time of year anyway."

"You have to go. Where will you buy the hinges for your gate? And for the drawbridge? No forge within a hundred leagues of your village can make them. You could use a few good swords too. I think," he continued now, looking me in the eye, "that it is time that you meet

King Bjornson. I knew his father, the old king, very well, that was before his time, but he is much like his father. He sees much that other men don't. He knows the power of runes and much more. You must meet him; a king for a friend can be useful. I hear too that he is now much more than the ruler of the Danes; other jarls of the north have kissed his arm ring."

The Family of Magic

That, indeed, is news. But how will I explain this to Astra? She will fret as she always does when I travel. Nor have I made such a long trip as this since I came from the Rus."

"Take her with you. The time of the year for raiding is now past. She
has a part to play in your future. A future that is very important to more than just yourself or your village. But I must leave you; I can go no farther."

"Goodbye, grandfather, but please tell me, is the hairy star a sign of doom?"

"When is it not? But Odin has not vouchsafed me that knowledge. Let no signs or omens keep you from your true purpose. Go to the Danes and tell their high king that an old man, a shade from years gone by, still remembers and honors the memory of his father. Above that, take no person at face value at court. Power and money attract more strange fish than can be accounted in the sea."

He looked me hard in the face for a moment, then laughed and waved his hand as he turned on his heel heading for a path that led across a grassy field. I was too stunned by all of this to say more. Later I would revile myself for not saying this or asking that. Such reproaches do no good, of course, but I find myself doing it anyway.

*

Six days after I had this dream, if a dream it was and not a vision, I was seated on the deck of a trading ship bound for the capital of the Danes. Next to me on the heaving deck was Astra, along with our oldest son Flosi. I had wanted to bring our oldest daughter Gudrin so she could see something of the world, but my wife wouldn't hear of it, claiming that the girl's health was too delicate. Unsaid was the fear of pirates and robbers. We took a sailboat from our village to west along the coast to where a group of wandering Franks, mixed with the assorted leavings of other tribes, had set up a thriving trading and fishing community. They were protected by several miles of mud flats and shoal waters, which only a shallow draft boat like ours could negotiate. This collection of dwellings, many just hovels, is called Vastardic, which I learned later was a corruption of the Frankish word for toothache; the reason for that is obscure. This distance wasn't far, but because of hostile currents, sand bars, and a myriad of islands, it took most of the day. The captain of this vessel was amazed at the speed we traveled; he had never seen such a consistent wind; of course, he knew nothing of my wife's abilities. Whenever the wind would begin to flag, her eyes would glaze over until the wind picked up. She got no complaint from me, for sailing at this time of the year, even on a sunny day, was cold. Astra, Flosi, and I shivered all the time, even though we were wrapped in layers of clothing. Our shivers amused the man who owned the boat as he sat at the tiller. At most, he considered this weather only a little bit chilly, and if the wind sliced through our garments, at least it was pointed in the right direction. At mid-afternoon, we sailed into the village of the sore teeth.

As we sat waiting for the headman, I couldn't help thinking about the past week's events. And I hoped that all would be well at home.

Before leaving, my preliminary plans were approved for the fortifications. The villagers were enthusiastic about them once I passed around a couple of chalk sketches I had made showing the gate with the flanking towers and another showing how it would look from the harbor. Once word had spread about this great fortress that even the Gods wouldn't be ashamed to live in, people began to gather tools and organize work crews. As in all communal projects, everyone would donate according to their rank, ability, and in some cases, their health. I knew their enthusiasm would cool along with the weather, but I didn't doubt their ability to stick with the plan. Hard work and adversity were their common lot and were fully anticipated. People didn't expect much from life, so they were seldom disappointed. The idea that their safety would depend on a wall of trees said a lot about the times I lived in. Was the world always like this, I wondered?

At length, a small group of men approached. We were armed; I had a sword in a scabbard hanging at my hip with its strap hanging over the opposite shoulder. Flosi had a long knife in a sheath at his waist, and there were knives that couldn't be seen, including a throwing knife, made deadly by her uncanny accuracy, strapped to Astra's left forearm. Even so, we couldn't be taken for anything but what we said we were, travelers in need of a ship. The sight of my silver coins had the desired effect. A deal was soon struck to take us to the Danes at Roskilde. We would leave the following day, weather permitting, which we knew it would. The owner of the vessel gave us shelter in his house at night and a very welcome hot meal. The food was good, and so was the information. The dark, dog-eared merchant, whose family came from a mountainous region south of the Franks, was no fool and told us honest opinions and shrewd guesses. We heard much about the newly married High King of the Danes, whose new Queen, Thyra, was reputed to be the most beautiful woman of the Frisians; she brought lands and much wealth with her dowry. The king's younger brothers and sisters had done well too. All had gained from prudent marriages that brought power, wealth, and connections to his house. He had even received the submission of the Jutes who lived nearby on the land that protruded far into the sea. They were warriors who held large estates and had many cattle. This made him even richer and more powerful. The Geats sent him rich presents, as did the coastal islands of Scandia who sent him ship supplies like whale hide cables and pitch. How long this federation would hold together was unknown, but for now, it was the most powerful in the world. But his brow clouded when the hairy star was mentioned; had we not seen that it now has a tail?

"I know nothing," he said as he nervously twirled the ends of his beard with his fingers. "But it is said that fell things happen. A trader from Hedeby swears that when he sailed through Kattegat last, they found bodies tied together floating; they had been hideously mutilated. Each one had a strange mark branded on their face," he paused to draw something on a piece of wood with ashes from the hearth on his finger, "I know the man. He never lies about things like this." I looked at the marks he made with the ashes, but they meant nothing to me. "They say too," he continued, "that people flee the lands where their fathers farmed for generations, all out of fear, but what they fear is not known. Others tell of great flocks of carrion birds that circle the fields and villages. I don't have to tell you what an evil omen that is. While others tell of strange roaring noises heard at night, such as trolls might make." At this, he made a quick sign against enchantment and grabbed the charms around his neck, which were many, and called upon all Gods everywhere to protect him from seeing trolls, wolves, unhappy spirits, or any other inhuman beasts, alive or dead. The rest of us joined him in that earnest plea. Later, Astra questioned me about trolls and mythical beasts as we lay in bed waiting for sleep. Of course, I had never seen one, nor knew anyone who had. I had always thought of them as interesting characters in the stories told in winter. For what it was worth, I gave her my opinion that the most dangerous creatures were the ones with two feet. But the image, if true, of people floating in the sea, murdered, tied together, and branded worried me.

We were up early the next morning, thankful we had spent the night in a warm bed without fleas. Our host, who owned the vessel we were to sail on, took us down the water's edge and introduced us to the captain, who came via a large flat-bottomed scow poled by a muscular slave. While our bags of clothing and other gear were being transferred to our vessel, we met the captain of the ship. He was a short and stocky Dane with a shaved head covered by tattoos that were skillfully done. It must have cost him a fair bit as I recognized a couple of runes that, if placed there by somebody of power, would rain burning sulfur on anyone who tried to kill him. I had never thought of offering that sort of service, but after seeing his man's head, it made me think. Would such things as runes on skin work? I put that thought away in my mind for another day. As far as his talk went, it was mainly speculation on the likelihood of favorable winds and the unpredictability of currents off the Danish coast. What he said, in essence, was that with fair winds and good luck, we'd be there soon; if not, the trip would take longer. When pressed, he opined that we would sail into the harbor of Roskilde sometime tomorrow afternoon if the Gods permitted. But because the entrance to the harbor, which was miles long, was on the west side of the city, we could easily take another day or two.

After hearing this helpful forecast, we boarded the skiff and made for the river, where our transportation awaited us. The ship was substantial in that it had a fine tall mast. Amidships, behind the mast, was a large tent that would provide shelter, especially at night, as it was too dangerous to put into land unless compelled to do so by bad weather. The ship was constructed, as near as I can tell, being no expert in building such vessels, by overlapping boards held fast to a frame by metal rivets. No doubt it could be used for any purpose, such as trade or raiding; it could hold at least thirty men, maybe more if the voyage was short. The ship had, as usual, a carved beast on the bow post and on the stern post a crudely carved phallus of strange proportions. Woven into the sail, which was raised as soon as we were pushed away from the dock, was what was supposed to have been Odin's eight-legged horse Sleipnir. What it looked like to me was a very unhappy-looking octopus.

The captain, Uwolafa, proved garrulous, so we listened to him in shifts. His crew of three, long used to his energetic tongue, were much the opposite. They had little to say about anything. No matter, their captain covered all subjects from news to tales to proper seamanship and speculations regarding the hairy star so clearly visible by night, the strange news from Scandia, and a marked increase in pirates, sometimes even small fleets of these dangerous thieves. He also talked of the doings at the court of the Danes. This was not all bad, for I picked some gems of information amongst the mental trash of a credulous sailor.

According to Uwolafa, the King of the Danes was renowned for his wisdom in counsel and battle skills. All the worthwhile people in that region paid homage to him, and his court was the center for many good things like song, poetry, and the production of skilled crafts of all kinds. But the rumors of strange goings on in Scandia now troubled the court. A ship had been sent to investigate but had yet to return. It was known, the captain said in a low voice, that certain evil men plotted against the King and sought his overthrow. Some so vile as to seek dark magic to use against him. But for himself, he appealed to the Gods for protection for the Danish King, whom he clearly held in high regard.

That day and the night that followed were uneventful, with fair winds pushing us along at a brisk pace, but the following morning, just as I awoke to piss, I heard a cry from the lookout. A boat that had been hidden behind a small island was now in apparent pursuit and, from the speed of their rising and falling oars, would be on us in a very few minutes. The captain let loose a fantastic volley of oaths and imprecations at the pirates who were over-hauling us and ordered the ship's weapons be brought out. He grabbed a bow with the intention of taking a few souls to the underworld with him as he stood there on the heaving deck calculating the distance. Doing so would not change the course of events; the pirate vessel was crowded with men, but he was not a man to die without a fight. But a strange thing happened just as he was about to let fly with the first arrow. A freak wind rose against the pursuing ship, followed by a sudden storm whose fury ripped the sail from their mast and filled half their vessel with water. The men on our ship were in complete disbelief as they watched the discomfited thugs bail water like madmen. One minute we were in mortal danger of being taken and murdered by pirates; the next, we were not. The situation was quite comical; the captain and crew looked like stunned ducks hit over the head with a stone.

One of the crew looked at Astra, quickly noting her glazed eyes and unnatural stiffness. He pointed to her after yelling out something unintelligible. Falling to his knees, he could only look at her and gibber like he had seen a ghost. The others were not far behind him in fear once they had comprehended what had happened. All of them shook in fear, even the captain, a veteran, he said, of many battles.

Gradually she returned to normal, although it took her much longer than usual. I believe that this was because she had never had her powers put to the test in real life, like a youth trained up in the practice yard with a sword and spear who never truly knows what he has until he faces a foe in battle. Seeing that she did not kill anyone with lightning bolts or shrivel them with curses, the crew came to their senses by degrees. The captain ordered wine for everyone and sat down with me, this time to listen, not talk, as I did some hurried explanation of her powers and their uses. The crew was still put out over the fact that they had a weather witch on board. But the fact that she had saved their lives was not wasted on them. The rest of our trip was uneventful, although the episode with the pirates put a curb on the captain's tongue. He and the crew were genuinely unnerved; no doubt, for years to come, they would have a tale to tell that, although true, would be considered just another sailor story. The late afternoon of the second day saw us on the island's far side, where the fortress and city of Roskilde were located.

As we hove into view of the city, we found the sight imposing. The entire wall that enclosed the dock was made of stone instead of wood. This represented an expense that only the wealthy and prosperous, or the greedy and extortionate, could afford. Even from a distance, the activity on the docks, the loading and unloading of goods, and the general level of activity bespoke a flourishing economy. No wonder the walls were so high and the towers so numerous. The mighty tower on the left would take fifty men or more to garrison the structure; something told me they could be found. Upon entering the harbor proper, we were met by a man in a boat rowed by a couple of slaves who, after conferring with the captain, pointed to a dock where we could tie up. No time was wasted by the sailors who wanted as little more to do with us as possible. In a matter of minutes, we were deposited on the dock with our belongings piled next to us.

A short time later, a cross-eyed official with the back of an ox who looked like an off-duty berserker, flanked by guards, asked our business. I told him that we came to buy weapons, various pieces of ironmongery, and cloth; this excited no interest in him, but when I told him that my trade was *Runemaster,* he gave me the searching stare of a fresh appraisal. I guessed that it got us better quarters. He then told us to wait where we were; he would send us a cart to haul our baggage, with an aside that no more than two coppers should be paid to the driver. I thanked him for his assistance, but when the cart arrived, I held three coppers in my hand as I plied the man, who had lived here all his life, with many questions. Some he could answer, some not, but my extra copper was nonetheless a good investment. He took us to the door at the rear of the palace, where a waiting guard showed us to our quarters. This seemed strangely efficient to me as one who had traveled much of the world without seeing much competence. Being given two rooms, even small rooms for only three people, was an extravagance that would have been unheard of elsewhere.

"They think highly of their king, which is a rarity in itself," said Astra, "most kings that I've heard of are known for having hearts as hard as the flints you use to carve your stones with."

"But don't kings want to be popular?" asked Flosi as he finished unpacking our travel bags."

"A few might," I considered, "but most would rather have your fear than your love. Rulers, for the most part, are a remorseless crew with big appetites that extend beyond the table." "Does he have children? Sons?" Asked Astra. "The more sons a king has, the more the people suffer after he dies. They quarrel over the inheritance, and the little people pay the butcher's bill."

"I've never heard of it put that way before, but you're right," I said as I changed my traveling boots for something more suitable for the indoors. "I wonder what he will do with his other women now that he has taken a Queen? The woman Thyra that he married won't stand for any rivals; the Frisian women of rank scorn men who take additional wives or concubines."

But further speculation was cut short by the appearance at our door of a well-dressed man, a slave judging from his iron collar, who brought us a tray of bread and meat and talked to us about where we should be and when. While he spoke, another couple of slaves appeared, similarly attired, with pitchers of water and cloths for washing and even more food and drink. Lastly, he showed us an old crone that would be stationed outside our door during daylight hours to see to our needs. He suggested that we bar the door at night and not wander around the palace, the palace corridors were patrolled at night, and the guards were always rude. We took the hint; we were being watched. That night not only was the door barred but small wooden wedges that my father had used in Rus so long ago were pushed in under the door as tight as they would fit. A small precaution, proper, but it would make the door very difficult to open without a lot of noise. The next morning, we were again served food in our room but told to have ourselves ready at any time for the king would soon be receiving visitors as soon as the press of business would allow, which was to a smirking Astra a sign that he was busy in his quarters with his wife. But to me, that was all to the good as a king in a good mood was a better person to meet than one who was not. We didn't have long to wait, though; just as we finished our food, bread, cheese, and apples, a bald man in a long black robe appeared at the door holding a long wooden staff tipped with an iron head of a dragon with deep-set ruby eyes.

"Let us take the long way; the servants are cleaning the floors now; you wouldn't want to get your shoes wet. I am told this is your first time here, and you are a master of runes. Very good, we like knowledgeable visitors to call on us. The King always seeks information on what is going on outside our borders."

"I've been told that the borders have been expanded recently due to the wisdom of those who seek shelter under the cloak of King Bjornson." I said as we entered the brisk and chill morning breeze.

"That is very true," he answered with a hint of a smile, "the world is uncertain, so people naturally adhere to those whose wise leadership and arms are strong enough to protect them. You will meet many people from all over while you are here as the King now receives gifts from many places."

"There is always wisdom in giving gifts to those who are strong enough to appreciate them," I replied. Apparently, that amused him, for he gave out a good laugh.

"You speak very well for a man who does not live here at the court."

"My father was the counselor of several warlords, one in Rus, the other east of here," I waved my hand in a direction that could have been east," I didn't know the reputation of the deceased Dane that my father once worked for so I thought it best not to bring up any names.

At last, we arrived at the front door; Astra and our son were very quiet and humble as custom dictated, while I strode forward with head erect, a smile on my face, and my back straight. I was led up to the throne where the King sat, with his wife seated next to him, talking to a small group of men who stood in front of him. After they were dismissed, the King glanced toward us, gestured with his hand, and looked us over. The court official thumped his staff on the ground and stated in a loud, clear voice, "Comes to us now, Master Arn and family from the shores of the Salt Sea past the Saxon coast. He is a master of runes and a man of reputation and power; he brings his wife and oldest son." At this point, my wife and son quickly fell to their knees, and I gave a low and respectful bow.

"Rise, my friends, well met Master Arn," said the King in a booming voice, "we are most glad to see you. Songs are sung here about your grandfather, who was a great friend of my father. He was a hero! A real hero! Not just some braggart who paid the bards to sing his praises. Now introduce me to your beautiful wife and your son."

"This, your highness is my wife Astra and my son Flosi; I have another son and two daughters at home."

"You must attend the feast tonight and tell me all about them and any news you might bring from your home." The King said as he carefully but kindly appraised us. "I have summoned our own Master of Runes, Master Steinson, to keep you company and to show you around the city. We have many fine merchants and craftsmen; whatever you want can be found here."

"Thank you, your highness; my wife has a long list of luxuries we can't buy at home. I'm sure the local merchants will be much richer for our visit."

We were then taken to some benches at the side of the hall near a fireplace, where we were given cups of wine and told to wait. I suspected, after looking around, that placement near a fire was a sign of rank, as was just about everything else in the palace. We didn't know for whom we waited but welcomed the opportunity to rest our feet. The hall was neither full nor empty; people kept appearing and disappearing either out the front entrance or through the dozen or more side entrances. We saw many slaves, some in rough worker garb and others in silk. There were also warriors, merchants, and many whose purposes we couldn't guess.

"I have never seen a king before," Astra said with eyes wide. "But if I didn't know that he was a king, I might have mistaken him for one of the Gods come down to walk among us. His chest is like that of a horse, and his arms are like those of the giants that the stories tell of. And his beard is the color of the gold cups he drinks from. As for his wife, she is much younger, of course, but they were right to call her beautiful."

"I think you are in love," I said, making Flosi laugh, "you talk like a dewy-eyed maiden who has never seen a real man before. But I will allow that he looks every inch a king. And he doesn't wear that absurd sort of crown that one sees on the old coins."

"Did you notice that he wears no gold? Only silver? His cup is gold, but none of his rings or bands are. Even that circlet that he wears on his brow is silver. But did you notice that stone in it? It seems to change color the longer that you look at it."

"Ever wonder why I take your mother along, Flosi? She sees much. That stone could be enchanted. I don't know for what purpose, but it looks expensive; perhaps it was paid for in blood besides coins. I suspect that its purpose will never be known to us. Those who own such baubles keep their properties a secret; that's part of the magic. If somebody knows the charm that you wear, they might be able to figure out how to defeat it."

"Will it give him protection against arrows? Or a knife thrown at him?" Asked my son with a puzzled look on his face.

"His guards are there for that. It is more likely to warn him if poison is present or a sorcerer is hidden in the robes of a serving man. In such a case, the stone may grow warm on his brow in warning. Or it could be something completely different, but the more I think of it, the more I am convinced it is a charm stone."

"After seeing his Queen, I can think of another enchantment that he might be under, a domestic sort," Astra said as she leaned closer to the fire. The room was warm enough, but it was drafty with everyone coming and going.

"No man will blame him for that," I said as we waited, "for she is a rare beauty. She holds herself as though she was born to be queen."

"She does indeed," Astra said as she rubbed her hands together, "It is true what they say, I think, about her hair being the most beautiful in the north."

"Except yours, of course," I said, earning me a playful elbow in my ribs.

At that point, we were interrupted by the arrival of, judging from his garb with symbols and letters embroidered on it, the Master of Runes at the Court of King Baldur Bjornson.

"Your reputation precedes you, Master Arn, and the stories about your grandfather, even if only half-true, showed a skill and power rarely seen in these parts or anywhere else, I would guess."

"I cannot say if the tales told of my grandfather are true or not, but he was, in certainty, a powerful man. But as the Runemaster for a powerful and rich ruler like King Bjornson, you must be a man of incredible power. A ruler like him would not have a novice in his employ." I bowed slightly as I said this; flattery is a universal protocol that should always be employed among the great, near great, or with those of great pretensions. I was put off, though, by the man's clothing which consisted of a long black robe with a high collar. The robe was embroidered with magical symbols and runes in various colors. His hat was also unusual; it looked like a small wooden box painted and polished, then decorated, on each of the four sides, with small silver metal fish jumping like they would if they were after a frog. This contraption was tied by silk ribbons in a bow under his chin. However, I determined to keep my opinions of this foolery to myself. No doubt he thought that he needed these strange pieces of garb to overawe the crasser of the commoners.

He led us out the front door to a nearby tavern on a side street closer to the docks. There were a few sailors here, the higher-ranked ones anyway; most of the customers seemed to be merchants and their guards, with a few who looked like craftsmen now coming for a mid-day meal. The staple served was fish soup and bread or fish fillets with bread, all served with a rich white cream. Master Steinson, a man of middling height and build but with an outstanding head of thick black hair that flowed over his collar, controlled the conversation and told us many witty stories about the goings on in court. Flosi was highly impressed, but my wife looked a trifle skeptical. I was skeptical, too, but when I tried to extend my senses to probe him, I found that he was strongly shielded; he had real magic hidden behind his easy banter and strange habiliments. I was relieved to learn later that he wore this peculiar uniform for special occasions only, which, as it turned out, included the meeting of my family and me. The food at the tavern was good, even if the menu was limited. The ale was excellent; it had a pleasant, slightly nutty taste. At this point, I began to press my brother in runes for information, starting with the most obvious matter; the hairy star we now see on every clear night.

"One hears many opinions concerning the meaning of that night visitor. Perhaps it is just the trick of a demon wanting to make us mad with all our guessing? I wish I had a brass coin for every possible explanation that is being talked about. But in truth," he said, looking at us one after the other, "I have no idea what it means. But I believe it is changing colors; it was pink, and now it's getting redder. A red star, it is often said in the old adages of our fathers, is an ill-omen. But let us talk of more happy subjects; tonight, you, Master Arn, will be invited to the great hall where you will feast on the King's pork, drink his mead, and hear stories true and not so true. Bards will sing, wise men will talk, and idiots will bark like dogs. And you, mistress Astra and young Flosi will go to the woman's hall where you will dine and meet the Queen and high-born ladies of the capital.

"It won't be as noisy," he said smiling, "but the company will be more civil and probably more intelligent. Don't worry, my young lad; there will be boys your age there as well; bring a few coins with you; usually, they tire of talk and would rather play at drafts."

That night I was escorted from our rooms to the main hall while my wife and son were packed off in the opposite direction. Flosi was inclined to be a little sulky at not being allowed to be with the men, but he was too young; he had not bedded a woman and fought in no battles; there would be time enough in his life for revelry. I was glad that I had brought my best clothing and a few rings and chains to wear for appearances separated the wealthy from the rabble in the minds of the worthy and their followers, especially their followers.

When I entered the room, an ancient man stood on a small, raised platform at the head of the room and was engaged in telling a story of some sort. Such entertainers were common among those who could afford them, for the winters were long and often dull. A man with a good, strong voice and a knack for telling a tale was always in demand. Such a person would typically stay at one hall for weeks or even months at a time until all had heard his stories several times.

I was seated at a bench near the front of the room between a couple of large men whose armbands proclaimed them as jarls who owned large estates and were the King's representatives. They were also expected to lead their men in battle. As both bore scars, it was safe to assume that they were not strangers to the shield wall; they paid me no mind, however, as they were both listening to the bard. As soon as a servant brought me meat, bread, and ale, I turned my ear to what the venerable man was saying in his virile cadenced voice:"

...Then Heimdahl, seeing this blew his horn. He blew it so long and hard that the birds' nests fell out of the trees. He blew it again until icicles hanging from the beards of the giants shattered, then he gave one more mighty blast that shook the squirrel Ratatoski loose from Yggdrasil, the Tree of Life. Then Odin, the All-Father, led the Gods out of the gate towards the great plain of Vigrid that stretched before Asgard. All the Gods followed him well-armed and earnest. Then came the victorious dead from out of Valhalla. Out of five hundred and forty doors, they came running; at each door came eight hundred in shining armor and shields, urged on by the Valkyrie who shouted encouragement to them: *shatter their skulls and let fly a storm of spears, soak the ground with their blood, and rend their limbs! No craven spirits are here; you are all heroes and brothers in death and blood. Let no monster live nor suffer an oath-breaking giant to breathe. Let all the big eaters taste a mouthful of the sword, spear, and axe.* Here the bard paused to drink from his cup and compose himself. In his mind's eye, I am sure that he and everyone in the room pictured themselves standing shoulder to shoulder with the Gods on that fateful day yet to come. The room was in total stillness; no sound was heard as he launched back into his rousing story.

"When they reached the plain before them, Odin ordered the line of battle, taking the middle spot for himself. He held the mighty spear Gungnir in his hand as he sat astride his huge eight-legged horse Sleipnir. His ring shirt was of the brightest silver; his shield shone like the sun. With him stood Vidarr, the vengeance-seeker who was so quick in battle that he was never cut, and Vali, who grew so fast to manhood. And, of course, there was Thor, the mightiest of Odin's children. With his gloves, he could always catch his hammer, Mjolnir. Today he rode in his chariot and wore his magical belt that doubled his powers. He was joined by his sons, the great Magni and the brave Modi. His daughter Thrud was also there, clad in the armor of a shield maiden. Even the God Bragi was there, the one whose voice is so pleasing because he has runes imprinted on his tongue. His wife Idune was there too, she of the silver voice, today she carried a silver sword.

"Odin, having ordered his forces according to his wisdom, now sent Freya forward to spy out the advancing horde of vile monsters, giants, trolls, wolfmen, bloodsuckers, and foul beings of all sorts. Not forgetting the ice monsters and poisonous snakes. They are getting close now but are hidden in a heavy mist. Freya will change to the shape of a falcon as she has so often done. As she flies far above the plain, Odin bangs his spear against his shield to signal to all that the battle will soon start. Soon a great clamor is raised by his forces, causing alarm and dismay among the advancing creatures. The surging line of battle now stretches many leagues on either side of the All-Father can no longer be restrained. At last, Odin lifts his spear and points the tip forward. Once more, Heimdall put his horn to his lips. Once more, the mighty trumpet's sound proves too much for the advancing horde as many fall to their knees whilst holding their head in their hands. The charge of the Gods is well-nigh unstoppable, yet the monsters still advance."

But the fate of Gods and the heroes that accompanied them was not to be revealed to me that day, for at this point, I felt a tap on my shoulder. A servant motioned me to follow him as he took me out of the great hall by a side door. Down a long corridor, I went to a stout wooden door. A knock was quickly answered by a man who was wiping his chin with a cloth, Master Steinson—this time without his robe of runes or his peculiar hat.

The Runemaster Chronicles

Steinson

A quick look at the room was enough to tell me that although his previous appearance might have been comical, at least to me, he was nonetheless high in the order of the King's servants. I could see through an open door into another room, where stood a bed, a real one, covered with blankets and embroidered pillows. His furniture was carved with many fanciful flowers and beasts, his table large enough for at least six to sit at. These things and the fine tapestries on the wall were more pleasing than even the richest of the Rus, who were the standard by which I judged things.

"I'm sorry that you missed the end of our bard's story. But let me tell you that it doesn't end well for anyone involved. The Gods get killed, their followers get killed, the frost giants get slaughtered, and everyone else, even the stars, dies violently. Out of the chaos, a new world is born without any guarantee that the inhabitants will be any more honest, just, kind or more intelligent, or less greedy than the people they just replaced. Anyway, be welcome in my humble quarters, be seated, and have some wine; there are also seedcakes here. Here at least, we can talk without being overheard."

"If these quarters are humble, then I should like to see the apartments of the wealthy; they must have gold chairs and ivory walls," I said as I sat at his table.

"The King," he said with a wry smile, "is generous to those who help him. Those who oppose him, however, reside either in the ground, the sea, or in his very uncomfortable prison. There has been no king like Bjornson," he said as he sat at the table across from me, "he works hard. He is everywhere, yet nowhere. The other day, I needed to see him and was told he was looking at a new horse in the stables. But when I arrived, he had gone to inspect a part of a seawall that had collapsed after a recent storm. But I missed him there as well. They told me that he had returned to the palace to see the representatives of the northern Franks about trade. Yet at the palace, they said he had taken the Franks to the hall of merchants, where I finally found him. By then, I was so exhausted that I could hardly recall why I wanted to see him in the first place."

"Such is the lot of those who serve energetic royalty," I observed as I tasted one of the cakes and found them quite good, "So you brought me here, away from the tales of valor and slaughter so dear to the hearts of the Danes to talk, what will we discuss?"

"You are very direct, so different from those I usually meet." Here he paused to pour us more wine into our silver cups. "But you might be surprised to know that we have been watching you for some time. You have much power, and your woman is a weather witch, a very potent combination of people, I must say. Ah, you are indeed surprised," he said, seeing how wide my eyes opened, "did you think that with your magical heritage and fame as a cutter of runes and caster of spells, you could remain unnoticed? You have been watched for a long time, and when we learned of your wife's power, you were brought under even closer scrutiny. The king pays attention to people like you, as he does to all those who have the power to either assist or thwart him. But have no fear; I told his majesty that I sensed no malevolent purpose in you."

"The King has asked about me?" I asked in a somewhat nervous voice. "He told me to *see to you*, which means *find out what he knows*."

"Knows about what?" I asked, bewildered by this. "I didn't think I was important enough to know much about anything."

"You know enough to start fortifying your little village," he said as he looked me in the eye, "you gave lessons to your lady in how to call forth storms, and you made a stone of singular power for the people of an unfriendly island. Yes, don't look so surprised; we had one or more people always watching you. You see, our King," he said earnestly, "soaks up information and news from afar like a drunkard drinks wine. He can never have enough; his spies can be found everywhere. Merchants, soldiers even those who shovel shit on the fields could be in his employ. It must be said, though, that he is frugal with sharing that information. He shares only what he must."

"Forgive me if I am wrong, but I think now I will hear some of that hoarded news. I believe that I am about to hear something unpleasant." "You think so?" he asked with one of his wry smiles.

"Yes, I do think so. Men do not call others to their quarters for a private meeting to tell them good news. That would have been done in the great hall amid backslapping and good cheer."

"Well, you are right. It does seem to be bad or at least unpleasant news. As you have hinted, there are fell things going on, not so far away from here either. We have heard rumors for a long time ago about things going on in Scandia. But the news was contradictory. Of course, there are always stories about unholy beasts and creatures. That is to be expected; we are a people of superstitions," he said with the wave of his hand, "yet people were so terrified that they were taking ship to other lands, anywhere they could find. So, we sent a ship up the west coast of Scandia in the spring to find out what was happening and heard nothing more until a few days ago. A trader found the ship we sent at the entrance to a long fjord." Here he stopped and poured himself more drink like a man steeling himself for a difficult task. Then he paused for a while as he struggled to find words. At length, he resumed his story.

"The ship had been purposely pulled up on the shore. The crew was found with their hands nailed to the oars. All were hacked and mutilated; some had their eyes plucked out, others had heads cut off, and some missed ears, noses, and other parts as well. From the expression on their faces, this might have been done with them still alive. The ship's carved dragon head had been cut off and replaced with a pig's head. Around the ship, inside and out, symbols were made in blood. But the men could neither read nor write, so I have no idea what runes were used. Or why."

"Are you certain they are runes?"

"Yes, the men, some of whom I knew, were familiar with the stones I helped raise. Of course, they couldn't read runes, but they knew what runes looked like. This news shocked all of us, even the King. But there were other things as well. It looked like they were killed elsewhere and brought back to the ship. No weapon was found, and a couple of them footwear was missing. Their bodies had been stripped of all valuables down to the last coin."

"I hardly know what to say. This is grim news indeed. But what can it mean?" I wondered aloud. "It was meant to send a message for one thing."

"You are right, I think," he mused, "why else spend the time and effort to put the ship where it would be found sooner than later? Why mutilate the bodies and then leave runes? This is not the work of a band of wild berserkers. Yes, you must be right; a message was intended, but to whom?"

"It must be the King," he replied, "if they captured these men, they would have known they were on a mission from King Bjornson. That could not be hidden for very long. But I say this; it would have taken at least a hundred good warriors to overwhelm these men. But where could ships and men be found in such a place?"

What about your neighbors, the Jutes? Or the Franks or the Frisians? There must be those among them who would wish to challenge King Bjornson?" "There is no shortage of strong men and big eaters who wish to sit on this throne. But if any of them were to try and organize such a raid, we would know it before they sailed out of the harbor.""Hmmm," I mused as I drank more wine, "an unknown enemy is the most dangerous. But I don't know what I can do to help the King; he is obviously a good man. Living in my little corner of the world, there is not much I can do, and I'm committed to assisting in building the defenses, which will take years."

Astra Storm Queen

"I don't think that you will be leaving in the near future. The King has told me that he requires your service. You can blame your grandfather; I was told that if you *were only a third part* of your ancestor, that would be a powerful addition to the King's forces. Well, we both know that you are more than that. Also, the power of your wife is greatly desirable; as far as we know, she is the only living storm witch. That fact," he continued in a low and earnest voice, "is something we need to keep to ourselves. If word got out, an enemy might try to kill or kidnap her; we must be careful of every word we say, so guard your tongue."

"But what about the goods that I came in search of? My children will worry if I don't return; they will think I've been captured by raiders or worse."

"No need to worry," he said as he pushed his chair back and crossed his legs, "we'll find a way to get word to your family and your village too. Or you're next of kin if the need should arise. You can get your iron gate handles and hinges made while you stay with us. The weather will soon turn cold; it's better if you winter here. Regarding weapons, I know the best people to buy from; I can help you in that matter, at least. Don't worry, my friend," he smirked, "the King knows how to reward good service. You will be a strong addition to our forces when we go to battle."

"A battle?"

"Yes, a battle. There is always a battle when a question of strength or destiny must be decided. The only question is against whom? Or rather, against what?"

That evening in bed, I had a lot to tell Astra before we found sleep.

Chapter Three
The Death of a Courtier

The condemned man was led out in chains to the small square on the north side of the palace. He tried to smile as a man happy in death, which is always more pleasing to the Gods who frowned on those who wept or cried for mercy. The executioner's assistant grabbed him by his ear and pulled him down to his knees before the chewed and blood-soaked tree stump that had often been employed as an executioner's block. It was announced that the man had been guilty of rape and murder and that the victim's family had chosen his death over blood money. The man shook his head when asked for his last words. At this, a foot was put on his back, forcing his head down, followed by a swift blow from a sword. The executioner briefly held up the head, spit on it, and tossed it away. By custom, his head, being that of a low criminal and not fit to grace the spikes on the entrance to the fortress, would be fed to pigs.

By now, the snow had begun to fall again. It was almost always snowing at the capital of the Danes, it seemed, and I was happy enough to go back inside. I was not here willingly, I found no pleasure in seeing such things, but members of the court, even minor ones like me, were expected to attend executions. It was thought, I supposed, that the sight of heads being lopped off would excite loyalty in people. I was glad that my son was not here to see it. He had met some of the local boys and had become quite popular. Today he was invited to the room behind the barracks where soldier's sons were roasting apples and drinking cider.

Master Steinson accompanied me. I was often in his company these days. Afterward, we headed for his quarters, where my wife was waiting; I nodded to the guard outside his door. All of us were guarded now, ever since the last day of Yole when the guards, who were rewarded with gold coins for their steadfast sobriety even in times of great feasting, apprehended a stranger they found wandering the halls. He refused to answer questions, so they locked him up until the morning when he could be properly questioned. When they came to his cell to fetch him for examination, he was found dead with a vile-smelling scum on his lips. Master Steinson called it poison, and I think he was right. I helped to examine the corpse. In a small bag that hung from his belt, we found a few copper coins, a flint, and a piece of iron for starting a fire but nothing else. On his upper arm, we saw a strange brand that Steinson determined was the Christian symbol, but inverted, for what purpose we couldn't imagine. This caused us both to wonder what we were dealing with; to brand somebody in a place that couldn't be seen was unusual. Only later did I recall seeing this mark before. The man we hired passage to Roskilde from had traced that same design with his finger in ashes when we stayed that night in his home. He said this mark was branded on the mutilated bodies found in the ocean. Also found was a small wooden box that was fastened to his belt. Inside was a strip of parchment with characters of a language written on it that neither of us could identify. We also found hidden pockets containing small knives, with a substance, probably poisonous, staining the blades. Nobody doubted that this was an assassin. But who was his target? Could he have hoped to get close enough to the King to wound him with a poison blade? Or was his target somebody else? I could not come to a conclusion about the matter, although Master Steinson thought it highly unlikely that this man could have ever got within striking distance of the King.

Yole had come and gone sixty days hence, so we were now at the end of the month of Dori, so naturally, we looked forward to warmer weather; we also thought of home. Word had been sent back to our village advising the family and our friends that we would be detained due to pressing work that the King had asked me to undertake. And as a symbol of the King's favor, the village was given an assortment of weapons which I'm sure was gratefully accepted. It was reported to me that the work was going forward, trees were being felled and hauled according to plan, and upon the arrival of warm weather, the walls would be started. I hoped that I would be home before the work became too far advanced as I had reservations about the ability of my neighbors to construct the defenses according to my plan. Astra chided me for fretting about a wooden wall. How could anyone build a wall the wrong way even if they tried? Her opinion of the villagers was much more optimistic than mine.

"An execution is a poor relish for our meal," admitted Steinson, with whom I have become quite friendly with during this time. Astra, too, had become fond of him; he treated her with great respect, and I think he genuinely admired her power and, quite possibly, her person. How deep and genuine his feeling for others extended remained to be seen. He was proud of his ability to make friends with many types of people. He knew how to flatter and to praise. Nor did he once show a gratuitous disrespect for those in the lower orders. This was very different from how some jarls treated their lackeys with frequent kicks and blows. Much of the face he showed the world was a sham, yet the man cannot be described as a fraud. His court costume, though, was a definite attempt to deceive. He joked about it to me, saying that he wore these things only to differentiate himself from those of the fighting class, which was just about everyone. Without this strange garb, he would be just another of the faceless crowd who vied for the king's attention at court.

"The Queen told me that the executions were once more numerous," said Astra as a servant brought her a plate of hot bread and honey. "She said the yard would be so full of blood that the onlookers got it on their feet. I can't see how that would be pleasant in the least."

"She's right," said Lord Steinson as he moved to sit beside her, "the blood payments stopped most of that. You may kill me if you have a hundred gold marks to pay for it. Before this, if I killed your father, then you would kill mine and perhaps a brother or sister for good measure, then my family would repay you in the same way, death for death." This was a shrewd move on the part of the King as it eliminated most clan warfare that exterminated whole families.

"The King was, I agree, very wise in doing this." As I tasted the stew, I said, "the treasury is helped, too, as the King gets a little token of coin when he approves all such transactions."

"You are quite right," laughed my colleague in runes, "nothing is free here except for the smell of the ocean and the shit the birds leave on the boats. Yet I'd wager those would be taxed too if only a way could be found to do it." This got a good chuckle from us, for the comment was not only witty but pretty accurate.

"The Queen told me an interesting story yesterday about King Redwald of the island Saxons. It's said he is the master of the best part of that country and that he has a large fleet. But if he has a large fleet, where does he sail to? I have not heard of his warships being seen in the Skaw, Kattegat, or anywhere else," my wife asked.

"He probably uses them to beat up on his neighbors," considered Steinson. "I have heard similar rumors that he is lucky in combat and very rich. You can be sure that our King has somebody at his court. It's good that you talk to the Queen," Steinson said as he helped himself to more of the rabbit stew we were having, "She knows more about the royal houses and wealthy families than anyone I ever met. Her knowledge is often better than what we can purchase from spies. You can believe me when I tell you we don't lack spies."

"You must be right, Master Steinson, for I think I found some of them." Astra paused to smile at Steinson's quizzical look, "I saw my second maid, the little pig Guri, sneaking into the quarters of Lothar Bentoar. No doubt to report gossip about us to him."

"I know the man," said Steinson with a laugh, "the old skunk lives in a small house across from the rear of the palace. You think that our tax collector is collecting more than just money? How do you know he is not just fucking her?" Asked Steinson after selecting a smile from his store of false looks.

"Ugh," Astra sniffed in disgust, "the idea of those two repulsive people lying naked next to each other is disgusting. But you know that it is common knowledge that a spear thrust years ago ended his ability to raise his exhausted stump. And besides, she wasn't in there long enough to satisfy his ancient lust, even if he had any. Out of curiosity, I watched his door from behind some barrels to see who else might visit. A little while later, I saw a boy I knew from the kitchens enter. And after he had gone, I saw a girl come; I didn't recognize her, but she was meanly dressed, so I thought she must be a servant of some sort as well. I suppose using servants is smart; they spy on their betters; as we know, treason is most often plotted among the wealthy, besides family members, of course."

"I guess that we'll all have to be more careful what we say to each other in front of the servants," our host said, looking at each other in turn. His smile was still on his lips, but I suspected my wife's comments unsettled him.

"You will have to tell your spies to be more careful," I said after the serving woman left the room.

"I'm not the master of spies, but I know who is, and a word might reach his ears. Tell no one about this, though." He said in a low voice, looking at us both in turn. "He won't be pleased; if Astra can see this, who else might have? Of course, I have no way of knowing what this man is up to, if anything," he said primly. "But if he is receiving reports of some kind, it is just pure laziness to have his people come to his door."

Following our meal, we decided to take a hike to exercise and alleviate the oppressive feeling of being kept in a cage like an animal by the miserable weather. The past ten days had been cold, windy, and snowy. Today it was merely cold, with only a light dusting of snow. We headed to the docks to see what we might see. It has been rumored that the King's new ship of war has been started, but I was skeptical about what kind of work could be done in these conditions. The shipyard was located on the far side of the harbor, where the land was very flat. Even at this distance, we could see dozens of ships lined up, all on wooden rollers. But hardly any workers; it was too cold to do any caulking, which was the most common chore in shipyards. The gap between the planks must be packed with fiber or roots and sealed with hot pitch to keep the water out. Of the king's new ship, we saw nothing.

"Well, this is a disappointment," said Steinson, "I thought they were further along. But they haven't even laid the keel and the mast block."

"I don't know much about ships," said Astra as she passed the empty spot where the ship of war was to be constructed, "but is this ship going to be special? What is the name they are going to give it?"

"I've heard it's to be named the *Silver Dragon*," I said as we walked along.

"I heard it's going to be called the *Long Wolf,*" said Steinson as he turned to look at the harbor, "but you can ask the King yourself tomorrow morning at the meeting. You are to come also, my lady. I greatly suspect," he continued as he turned to look around, apparently to make sure nobody was near us, "that we will be talking about the problems north of us. The problem that resulted in that ship of death I told you about. So tonight, when we celebrate the Feast of Torrablot, don't drink too much wine. You will need to keep your wits about you. And lady Astra, please wear a hooded coat; we don't need to advertise that you will be with us. I will come early for you so be ready. I don't know where we will meet yet, and I won't until the morning."

"A high honor, my love; not many women have such influence that they attend the secret consultations of the King."

"Hah, you'd be surprised what he talks to his wife about. I hear plenty. But nothing about this particular problem, come to think, but what *IS* the problem, anyway? All I know for sure is some tall stories and a ship of slaughtered men."

"The King has many sources of information that are not available to us. Anyway, it is useless to guess." I replied.

"We'll be at the feast, of course, but won't stay late," I said as I turned to look at Steinson. For myself, I looked upon the honoring of the winter spirits as a duty, not something enjoyable, for we see far too much of these frozen entities with their cold and snow in the north.

"This festival meant more when we were home in our own house." Astra said as we walked along, "I would take my daughter with me and put seedcakes outside for the demon spirits of the cold. It was only a sign of respect. Then the family would have a good hot meal and play some games. I'll go too, of course; for a woman to be invited is an honor, I suppose. But maybe it's one of those honors to be avoided. Being here at court for all these weeks has made me wary of any honors or distinctions, for all such things require a price to be paid."

"You learn quickly, my lady," smiled Master Steinson, "to have one's head held higher than the others is a distinction, that is certain.

But it is a fact that the higher the head, the closer it is to the executioner's sword."

We walked back to the palace in silence, each of us wrapped in our thoughts. My thoughts were full of worry. I had spoken little to the King since my arrival, but I got the feeling that he got frequent reports concerning me; Astra was mentioned, no doubt. Early on, Master Steinson asked for my help on the plans for the new palace, one built of stone, not wood; in that particular matter, I was able to make a genuine contribution since I had seen many such places in parts of the world, even the wondrous buildings such as those found at the entrance to the Black Sea. Master Steinson was good with numbers, so we worked on calculating the number of laborers needed in so many days to complete a task and the type and quantity of the materials required. My sketches of how the new palace would look were eagerly passed from hand to hand. The beauty of the design was praised, but to me, it was just a large and fancy fortification. However, nothing would be done soon; it would take a year or more to get sufficient cut stone from the quarries.

That night we went, along with Flosi, to the great hall; due to the nature of the feast, celebrating the spirits of the winter, there were no heroic tales or clashing of mugs upon the table. We ate pork and foul, drank cups of mead together, pledged each other good fortune, an early spring, and made our way back to our quarters. Astra sprinkled flour on the small altar near the door as we entered; she was diligent about paying homage to the Gods. But we wasted no time diving under the heavy wool blankets for warmth. Soon our minds drifted away after thinking about our children, some far away, and what the meeting with the king might bring. But the morrow came all too soon to suit the likes of me, who found the warmth of the blankets and the softness of Astra's skin next to mine very enticing.

It was, however, later than our usual rising time, so it was no wonder that the servants began to beat on the door. There was nothing for it other than to get up and let them in. Several women came in, some scurrying to bring pitchers of hot water and towels, others to revive the fire and bring food and drink. They were all very efficient; not even the chamber pot was overlooked. We were advised to dress warmly, no doubt to meet with the King, but we wondered why we needed guards;

two were stationed outside our door. A while later, just long enough to dress and eat, we heard a quick knock on the door. A guard stuck his head in and told us that we should put on our warmest cloaks and accompany them to the rear door of the palace. Here two sleighs awaited us; one to ride in and the other for our possessions. All of this was much to our astonishment, and I harbored serious doubts about meeting with the king and his advisers; something was very wrong. I had many questions at this point, but the stern faces of the servants made me think that now was not the time for talk.

Still, this was a novelty because none of us had ever ridden in a sleigh. As soon as our clothing and other gear were stowed away in the second sleigh, we were off. The expert flick of the whip over the heads of the three strong ponies, shod for ice, signaled our start. Furs were provided to pull over our legs, so I was soon very comfortable except for the tip of my nose. Probably more comfortable than the four guards who trailed behind the sleighs on horseback.

We followed a road that led out from the rear of the palace and through the fortification gate; soon, we left the road heading north across several broad fields to get to a river. Here we turned east along this stretch of frozen water, which made a convenient highway this time of the year. Judging from the many tracks, others, too, had taken advantage of this winter road. We continued on this route for a considerable distance, taking us into the late morning. At length, the driver called out to the horses and flicked the whip to the right. At this point, we launched up a bank and were once more among the farm fields. Here we could see in the distance a collection of buildings that included a large farmhouse. There were fresh tracks of both horse and sleigh that told me that it must be occupied. As we got closer, I could see smoke that no doubt came from a fire. Astra and I wondered greatly at this while our son, being unused to the ways of the world, thought that we were on some pleasure excursion. His mother and I had other expectations, none of which involved pleasure. I was pretty sure we had not been hauled all this way into the interior of the farming country to be slain; that would make no sense. But in a world ruled by treachery, deceit, dishonor, greed, and coveting, it makes sense to reserve judgment.

The house was typical of the kind of residence favored by the sturdy farmers of the Danes. They lived all in a heap with their extended families, servants, and slaves. The house was long, low, and had a thickly thatched roof. As it turned out, the King owned this house and used it as a hunting lodge when he felt the urge to track the wild boar who roamed the nearby hills and woods. Usually, at this time of the year, it stood empty. Today though, several people rose to greet us as we made our way in through the narrow door into the main hall, where a fire was burning brightly in the center of the room. The smoke stung my eyes at first; this was one of those buildings that didn't have a chimney, only a hole in the ceiling to allow the smoke to escape. The glass windows were few and small. Most of the light came from the fireplace or small lamps that burned tallow that gave off as much smoke as light. This was far inferior to the shark liver oil we burned in our lamps at home. I knew from experience that the toilet facilities would be a wooden seat over a bucket. Spending time in the relative luxury of the palace had spoiled us. I had little time to think about the deficiencies of Danish dwellings, for as my eyes cleared, I saw Master Steinson standing in front of me, holding out a flagon of heated wine. He poured us each a cup, for which we were very thankful. Behind him, I saw some men sitting on benches pulled near the fire. Servants bustled about bringing in our things from the sleigh while others brought in wood.

    "Well met, my friends," said Steinson taking Astra and me by the hand and pulling us towards the fire, "no doubt you are wondering why you were hauled from your comfortable beds in the palace and taken so far into the countryside. I'm sure you expected a meeting with the King, that will come but when I can't say. You must understand that he is watched by eyes that are not always friendly. So, I decided to make a last-minute change in our plans. Today we meet to exchange information and to form a basis for future action. And also get you from out of the palace to somewhere safer."

    "Where can be safer than the palace?" I asked. "My reasons for moving you here will be explained," said Master Steinson as he turned round to address everyone present, "let us pass the wine around, and everyone be sure to get a full cup since I must soon send the servants away. There are things to be spoken that are not for their ears. All of these are from the nearby village, who probably have no idea who we are. But in dangerous times, we can't take chances. So here, Lady Astra, hand the wine around before it gets cold. Be seated, friend Arn; warm yourself at the fire as I introduce you to our friends."

As he said this, he dragged a couple of high-backed wooden chairs forward; soon, we were warming our toes at the edge of the fire; Flosi made do with a stool and sat behind us.

"Master Arn," he continued, "is an artisan of the ancient craft of runes, and his learning has encompassed many areas of magic and power. He comes from a line of powerful magical practitioners. His grandfather is the man who killed the vile necromancer during the time of the old king."

When this somewhat intimidating introduction was finished, he resumed his seat across the fire from us. With a languid hand, he motioned to a heavy, bull-necked, bald man with a thick drooping black mustache who sat on his right. "This fine specimen of a fighting man is Master Bormo, head of the king's household staff. He is also the head of the king's spies and, if needed, assassins."

"There are those dead because of me; there is no doubt of it," the heavy man chuckled, "not all warriors stand in the shield wall. I made a deal with Odin long ago; he has promised me a seat in Valhalla." Others laughed at this, but not being in on the joke, I held my peace.

"But will there be enough Valkyrie to haul your fat carcass all the way to Asgard? They might get tired." At this, everyone laughed again, especially the man who was the target of this rude jape.

"Now I must introduce a man so much smaller than Master Bormo that by comparison, he is just a shade or, at most, a sprite." Here Steinson gave his trademark thin smile, "meet Master Hagala Nilsson, head of the household horse and all communications. If you need a message delivered anywhere in the nine worlds, he's your man." At this, a short, thin man in high black leather boots, a mop of unruly flaxen hair on his head, and a wispy reddish beard stood up and gave a short bow. "I should say," Steinson said after the diminutive man resumed his seat, "that Hagala has defeated men much bigger than you would suppose at the dinner table. His small frame won't hold enough to smother his appetite."

"This man lurking over here across from you is the King's man of coin. He requires more magic than anyone else in the kingdom as he is sometimes asked to get gold and silver out of an empty treasury, meet the thrice worthy and often damned Nakdan Thorson." Here an older, nondescript man with grey hair and beard waved a hand in our direction and then stuck his nose back into his tall cup of drink.

"Last of all," continued Steinson, "in this conclave of those who serve is the hard and often bitten Laukaz Bloodaxe, head of the palace guard and all foot soldiers on the main island." At this, a tall, lank man with a partly shaved head, long beard, and heavily inked neck and face stood and bowed. But did I say last? Forgive me, for we have one more important person, I should say a very important person, to introduce," Steinson said as he turned to his side and motioned a man forward. The man rose and dragged his chair closer to the fire before nodding to the assembled people who looked at him; some smiled in recognition. He was a distinguished-looking man of indeterminate age with a short beard, long mustaches, and snowy hair. His black tunic, covered with a loose grey coat, was of an older military style. Upon his hands were silver rings set with precious stones and many inked designs on his forearms. Around his neck hung a heavy gold chain that carried a small hammer and other tokens of the Gods.

"My apologies for being here, my lords," the man said without waiting for an introduction from Steinson. "I should have been in Valhalla long ago. I did my duty in no less than five major battles, but death would not have me! Many others who stood near me in the shield wall died with a weapon in their hands, but not me, no matter how far I pressed forward in the fray. You may ask your grandfather if you should talk to his ghost, Master Arn, about how I fought when we overthrew the unholy magician who called forth the naked dead to battle. I know some don't believe such things, but they were true enough, as this young man knows. Yes, Arn, you saw his mark on my arm, didn't you," he said while pointing a finger to his wrist where several runes could be seen, "Well, I was proud enough to put his name there. Gudgaest was more than a mighty enchanter; he was a perfect friend; let us hope you have some small part of his strength in you."

"You can only be Jarl Hakon Harefoot," I replied as I rose out of my chair in respect for him. "I praise the Gods for sparing you so we could finally meet. My grandfather told me of you many times. He spoke of your honor, honesty, intelligence, and the strength of your arm. All lift our glasses to the Jarl's honor, and may he live to stand once more among us in battle." This impromptu speech went over well. Astra took this opportunity to gain favor by refilling drinks from a pitcher since the servants had all been sent away.

As soon as Astra resumed her seat, Steinson called for quiet. "As you may have gathered, we have not met here to track down the King's boars that are by now living in deep holes in the sides of hills. They are welcome to stay there as far as I'm concerned."

"They were always safe enough from your spear anyway," said the master of coin. There were smiles at this; perhaps Steinson didn't shine in hunting.

"I never found the wild pigs as tasty as the domestic ones, and I was never taught the proper way of throwing a spear. I learned only how to toss knives." At this, he pulled a knife out of a sheath hidden beneath his cloak and threw it into a beam twenty feet away in less time than it would take to sneeze. The knife quivered in the post for several long seconds before anyone could take a breath. As the man walked over to retrieve his knife, the room was dead quiet. I felt that a message had just been delivered to all who might think he was an easy mark.

"Remind me never to get on your bad side," said Bormo, "you threw that hard enough to penetrate my bearskin coat." At this, Master Steinson chuckled easily with the confidence of a man who could plant the same knife in a man's throat at twice the distance.

"This exhibition of your skill is impressive, but did we need to come so far to see it?" Asked Nakdan Thorson as he stared moodily into the depths of his cup.

"I must agree with the coin hoarder," said the warrior Laukaz Bloodaxe, "Let's get to the point of this meeting here where only snow hares can be found on these wind-swept fields at this time of year."

"Except for Master Arn and his wife, I can say that we have known each other for some time. I have known Jarl Hakon so long I can remember him before he had grey hair."

"And much more of it," quipped the old Jarl.

"I will try to get to the point as soon as I can find it," Steinson said as he stroked his beard in thought, "but it is a fact that the kingdom, the King, and people in this very room are in danger. From whom we don't know yet, there are signs and clues. Yesterday our new friends here, Master Arn and his woman Astra were nearly killed by poison." He said, turning his shoulder around to face us. "Yes, your midday meal would have been your last, except I took the precaution of having your food secretly tasted without your knowledge. I can see that this is a shock to you, but I can tell you by the hammer that what I say is true. The crone who served your food always made sure to taste your food. She took a spoonful of pottage from the tray as she left the kitchen, she was soon on her knees, retching. She lived, but only because she filled herself with bread fresh from the kitchen, which absorbed most of the poison before it could kill her. I think anyone else would have soon died, but this woman was a tough old bird who worked for me for years. I started this precaution after the stranger was captured after the Feast of Yole. As you remember, that was a very suspicious incident."

At this, there was a long silence, after which Steinson took a deep pull on his cup, "There is more, the kitchen staff was questioned after the near death of the old woman. They seemed genuinely upset, as they had been together for a long time, except for one man, a cook named Clemon, who claimed that he had escaped from the pirates who ply the sea west of the Jutes. He was good at his trade and kept his mouth shut. He came to us, I should say, about a year ago, but following the confusion that took place with the sudden illness of old Friggia, he disappeared. The entire palace and fortress were ransacked, but nobody had seen him. He seldom mixed with the other servants. His life was so quiet as to make him almost invisible."

"Why should anyone want to kill us? We are new here, and few know anything about us." I said half to myself.

"You give yourself little credit; you have reputation enough to interest those who keep watch on the court and the people in it. I expect we'll find this man; I don't think he had time to escape the city. Whether or not he will be alive when found is another matter."

"I would be a liar if I said that your words didn't trouble me," said Lukasz, "there are few that I fear in outright battle, but an assassin, one who would stoop to poison, is another matter entirely."

"I wish assassins would do their work in warmer weather; attempting to kill a rune cutter at this time of the year shows a lack of regard for our comfort," said Hagala Nilsson with a slight grin on his face, "we should be like our jarls who are at home with their wives making more sons at this time of year. So why are we here? Murder has been attempted, but I don't know what I can do about it."

"I agree, that is where I should be, at home with my wives helping to populate Daneland with more copies of myself," said Jarl Hakon getting a few laughs from around the fire. Only later did I learn that he had recently took a third wife, one very much younger than himself. "But Master Steinson must have his reasons for calling us together, out in the barren fields away from the King's food and drink; let us hear him." "As you recall, we caught a stranger wandering the halls after the Yole Feast." Said Steinson as he looked around the room, "He carried a message that none of us could identify. It was a language used in olden times by the southern people who make that fine oil to cook with. It is said that at one time, they ruled most of the world. I learned this very recently from a trader who was bound to the Christians as a boy with the intention of making him one of their priests. He learned their language and teachings, but he ran away; he wanted women, not the scrawny bare asses of boys. When I showed him this, he knew what it was right away; he called it *Latin*. But he said the writing was wrong somehow. He studied for a while; then, he discovered there was a hidden meaning. It was the same writing the priests used to send messages to each other without the novices being able to read them. For a few coins, he was soon able to read the message for me. It said: *Set fire to palace--kill Arn-- see the old man for money.* Of course, we have no idea who this old man is, but we now know the target."

"We have a snake in our garden, one with a poisonous bite. There must be more to this story." Laukaz said as he leaned forward and put his chin in his hand.

"Do you think, Master Steinson," asked the old Jarl, "that this is in some way connected to the things which are going on in western Scandia? All of us know the fate of the ship that the King sent to investigate the strange rumors and the terrible and unnatural deaths of the crew."

"Who can say for sure? But the King has his suspicions--all news, what little there is, is bad. No merchant will go anywhere near that fjord. I have talked to all who have information or claim to have knowledge, but the stories are contradictory and, of course, frightening. Regardless of the tales that men tell, people are running from their farms as fast as their legs or ships or horses will carry them. Wolves on their heels couldn't drive them any faster."

"The King is right to be suspicious, Master Steinson," replied the Jarl, "kings who are not suspicious don't remain king for very long in my experience. This reminds me of a time long ago when another unnatural evil came to plague us. It was your grandfather, Master Arn, Gudgaest, a mighty man and most worthy friend, who defeated an evil devil-man whose knowledge of the unseen forces caused the death of many innocent people, thrall and thane alike. No doubt he told you that story many times."

"Yes, he did tell me the story," I replied, but not admitting that I was told it during a dream, "and it was frightening enough to freeze the mead in Odin's cup." Here there were calls for me to recount the story, for although the meat of the story was generally known, they wanted to hear it straight from a blood descendant. I have prided myself on having a certain gift for telling stories; I learned this art from my father, who was one of the best at that sort of thing. However, since I was not telling the history of the crazed wizard to an audience in a great hall, I declined to use heroic language and recounted the facts in a straightforward manner. A long uncomfortable silence followed my narrative. Everyone looked at each other without speaking; finally, Bormo spoke up.

"The implication that this previous evil has been in some way revived, most likely by the apprentice to this necromancer, is hard to avoid. But it's only a guess; we don't know what is going on or how to counter it. But nobody can think on an empty stomach, so let us call the servants back and have some food, and then we can talk a bit more.

"This suggestion fell on fertile ground. Soon we were forced to back away from the circular hearth as the servants started cooking. This gave me a little time to talk with Astra, who was very put out about the attempted assassination; Flosi couldn't get over it either. At some level, we were all of the opinion that we were out of our depth. As for my apprehensions concerning the toilet facilities, they were fully justified.

At length, when all had enough bread, fried fish, and eel pie to fill their bellies, the servants were once more dismissed. The assembled high heads in Dane land then sipped wine and tried to grapple with the problem at hand. Words of wisdom were slow in coming, however.

"What to do?" asked Jarl Hansson to nobody in particular.

"We can't just send another ship to find out what's happening. That was tried, and all we got was a boatload of corpses. Good men that we could scarce afford to lose." said Steinson with a frown as he tossed a stick into the fire.

"That part of Scandia is not overly populated to the best of my knowledge," mused Jarl Hansson, "maybe a stronger force than just a single ship. Say, six or seven good ships. That would be enough to handle any armed force we are likely to meet. Even if some sorcerer were able to raise the dead, how many could he find?"

"Maybe you have a good idea, but I would like to take ten ships," said Laukaz as he cleaned his nails with a small knife, "better to have too many men than too few.

"I would counsel against it," said Jarl Hansson, "everyone else should be against it too. There is much more to lose than we have to gain. No, the King must stay here and not go on an adventure of this sort. How do we know another old trick won't be used? The one where the King's strength is drawn out, not to be destroyed but to be led on a chase after wild geese? And while his forces are gone, the capital is attacked and captured. All of us know that has been done before."

"Has anyone thought of doing nothing and staying at home? How do we know that this, whatever it is, that is causing so much trouble, wherever this is going on, won't just go away on its own? Maybe the situation calls for a tonic of doing nothing at all. As far as the intrigue in the palace goes, it seems to have all been directed at Master Arn for what purpose we don't know. It may be connected to the problem that we might have in Scandia, but probably not," thus spoke Nakdan Thorson, keeper of the king's treasure.

"I have thought of that too," replied Steinson, "but I don't think for an instant that this is just some minor matter that could blow over like a quick storm in spring. We have here powerful weapons, so powerful that some enemy tried to deny them to us. I speak here of Master Arn and his wonderful wife. If demons stick their heads up in Scandia, we might end up someday with a whole nest of them to deal with; no, we must strike. But where and how may take a great deal of thought."

"Nor should we forget about the traitor mentioned on that parchment," said Jarl Hansson, "that could be anyone; an artisan, a soldier, or even a person of quality."

"I would say especially people of quality, given our history of treachery," replied Steinson. Nobody disagreed with this assessment. "But we need not come to a decision today. We will meet again and decide the matter; perhaps more will be revealed by then. At any rate, we must keep quiet about this meeting. We should all put our minds to work on the problem of what is to be done and look for my summons. Master Bormo, your spies must work harder, or you must hire more of them." This received a nod of grumpy agreement from Nakdan; more expense was the last thing he wanted, with the cost of a new palace hanging over his head. How much money the King had was a closely guarded secret, but looking at the number of the King's retainers, servants, and hangers-on who needed to be fed, clothed, and sometimes paid meant large expenses.

"Then we should be off, the days are still short, and I want to be back at the fortress before dark. I'll send somebody to get the horses ready. As for you, my friends," Steinson said in a low, conspiratorial voice after he had led us over to a corner, "I hope that you find these quarters suitable. They are not as comfortable as those in the palace, I know. Still, you'll be much safer. You will find your possessions and clothing behind that door," he said pointing, "We are leaving four soldiers to guard you and another four servants. The headman in the village, on the other side of the hill," Here he motioned with his hand to the west of us, "is trustworthy; at least, I hope he is. He has orders to keep strangers away from this farm. And so, my friends, I'll look in on you when time and weather allow. Until then, may the Gods protect you!" Then he was off, leaving us standing there still somewhat bewildered by the events of the day.

"This place is terrible," said Astra as she stared at the soot-covered rafters. "We're likely to freeze to death in here; I can almost see my breath. What will it be tonight when the fire dies, and the wind howls?"

"I hope we have plenty of firewood and furs to sleep under." As I said this, I looked around this cheerless room in distaste. Flosi, too, made his displeasure known. There would be little to do here; he would miss his new friends. To make matters worse, there could be weeks of snowy weather ahead of us. What could we do other than make the best of it?

The next few days tested our physical and mental stamina. Perhaps I had been spoiled, for even in the farthest reaches of Rus, we lived in better lodging than these. Astra, however, had been raised in a house much like this one, only smaller. Flosi, even with the energy of youth, disliked it; he had never been in a house before without a proper chimney or bed. What passed for beds here was a layer of fresh straw that had been evened enough to get the worst lumps out. Yet all of this was the rule among the Danes, and I suppose the other tribes and kingdoms as well. We were lucky we didn't have to share our building with the animals as many poor farmers did. It was not uncommon for a farmer to be awakened in the morning by a nuzzle from a goat.

Our servants did their best, but they were not trained servants. They were maids whose main job had been to milk cows and chop wood, save for one old crone who knew how to cook. She did well enough but only knew how to make a few very basic dishes like salt fish and baked black bread. After eating a piece of her thick, heavy bread, I felt like I had swallowed a rock.

On Thor's day, we had a visitor at mid-morning. By this time, we were very bored, and anyone would have been welcome, save tax collectors and assassins. A guard came and told us that a sled was approaching, accompanied by men on horses. They had been keeping watch from the barn's second story that stood immediately behind the house. Their situation couldn't be called comfortable, but thanks to Steinson, they had plenty to eat and drink. Smoked ham cooked over the open fire washed down with good mead went a long way towards keeping them satisfied. The barn also contained enough hay for them to burrow into at night, so they were no worse off than we were.

As it turned out, the man in the sled next to the driver was the old Jarl Hakon, followed by a couple of his men. This was a welcome sight indeed. The three of us tumbled out the low door into the overcast sky, a common sight this time of year. Actually, it was hardly any colder outside than it was within, and the air was much fresher. His men went off with our guards, who were told to share their fire and wine with them. The old Jarl, wrapped in a coat of wolf pelts, embraced us and bid Flosi bring in a bag of presents that he had brought. This included a large piece of smoked venison which was very welcome. Another gift was an excellent drink made of double-fermented wine of great strength. We all took a sip and felt the warmth flow through our bodies. He warned us against drinking too much of it at one time; the drink was so powerful that you could forget the cold, take off your clothes and sleep like a drunken hog until you froze to death.

We went inside, where the servants served us much milder mead to drink and some cakes made of very tough dough. There were brown spots in it that Flosi later insisted were bits of owl dung. Anyway, we sat and talked of the latest gossip from the palace; when the news was exhausted, which didn't take long for not a lot took place in winter except for the never-ending work of keeping fed and warm, the tough old Jarl leaned forward and smiled.

"I'm glad to see that you are making the best of things," he said after taking a long drink from his cup, "this building is very old, built in the time of Wolf Sword the Tall, so they say, old as I am he lived long before I was born. You may be surprised to hear that I was in this same house many years ago."

"That indeed would surprise me," I said, "For I know, good Jarl, that you are not from these parts." "Indeed, I am not from here, but many years ago, long before I was Jarl, I was a young ship captain under the old king. I sailed out of Roskilde with the fleet going through Kattegat down to punish the Franks with whom we were fighting at that time. We were just a small ship, scarce twenty fighting men, in the tail of a mighty fleet when a storm suddenly struck, and contrary winds drove us back to almost where we started. To make matters worse, a ship of pirates from one of the many islands of west Scandia happened upon us as we lay trapped against a lee shore. They had a large ship, crowded with men; I decided that if I couldn't save the ship, I would at least try to save the crew, so I ran my ship onto a beach, where I told my men to scatter and save themselves, my men heeded my advice except for a couple of stubborn warriors who wouldn't run, they were outnumbered and beaten down like dogs. But most escaped; I was wounded with a cut on my shoulder and an arrow in my leg. If I hadn't been found by an old woodcutter who put me in his cart and hauled me a good way inland, I would have been slaughtered too. He took me to a farmhouse, as it turned out, the very one that I am sitting in now, sorely wounded; I could have either died from loss of blood or infection. The woman of the house and her husband, an old soldier, knew enough about wounds and healing to save my life. They got much silver coin afterward as I was very much in their debt. But friend Arn," he said, putting his hand on my arm, "you should have seen me back then. I had arms so big and strong that maidens got weak in the knees just looking at them."

"You are still strong, my Jarl. May your strength never be less," I replied as I refilled his cup with wine.

"I may have reason to test it one more time before I leave this world. If we take action and go north, I expect to be asked to lead it."

"But that would be something you want, isn't it?" asked Astra.

"That is true, my dear," said the old warrior turning towards her, "I do indeed want to stand once more in the shield wall. But not for a trivial reason; I don't want young men to die with me for foolish vanity or to hear the bards sing my praises. Boys might think that all of war is glory," he continued as he glanced at Flosi, "but the story I just told was to make a point. The point is that just because you are brave and skillful, things can, and sometimes do, turn out badly. Many songs were sung to honor the old King and his victory, but the lost ship earned no praise."

"But doesn't the All-Father favor bold men of honor?" asked my son.

"Odin decides many things according to wisdom, but it's his wisdom, not ours. Also, I believe that in many matters, the Gods don't take sides. I suspect they just sit and watch us while they drink their golden ale. Or perhaps they make wagers on the outcome." The old man said with a laugh.

"Has our future action then been decided?" I asked.

"Nothing has been decided for sure. Opinion is divided and hesitant, I might say; some claim that we should do nothing and take the warning of the ship and its butchered men as an omen of that. Others say that the forces of evil are on the march in Scandia. If we wait, they could grow strong enough in time to overwhelm us. All agree that it could be a trap; our enemies are always thinking of ways to trick us somehow. Yet no king can allow fear of a trap or treachery as a reason to stay holed up like a fox in a den. Being either too timid or too bold has cost many a king his crown and his life; as in many problems, the arguments are almost evenly balanced."

"So, what will the King do if his councilors cannot agree among themselves?" asked Astra.

"They seldom do agree; most of the time, the King is presented with differing proposals. In the end, he must decide what to do. But knowing the King as I do," he said while stroking his beard in thought. "I believe he will not let this sore fester; no, he'll act. The only question is, how hard should he strike? We need to find out just what is going on inside that fjord. Ships will have to be sent, but how many? Will we find crews to fight what could well be the apprentice to the old necromancer that was overthrown in your grandfather's time? Men fear magic more than a spear or sword."

"I would send ten ships with as many men as can be put on board," said Flosi. "Let my father send lightning bolts to roast out their eyes."
"No doubt you would then chase the ones left with Odin's spear!" Here the old man gave a broad smile, "I was young once, too, and thought that I could slay dragons. You'll get your chance, but you must put more time into practicing with the other boys. Every morning you should be behind the barracks learning how to use weapons. Be sure that you attend; if anyone gives you trouble about it, mention my name."

"I can't go anywhere stuck out here. I swear that I hear wolves at night. When will we go back?"

"Soon, boy, very soon," he said as he rose, "you'll be returning soon. We hired some more guards and others to help watch. Also, we have changed things around so that our watchers will not be so easily seen when they give their reports to their superiors. Master Bormo was very much put out when he learned that Astra was able to detect his creatures entering the tax collector's house. Steinson was upset as well." Here he paused to chuckle as he got an obvious pleasure from the discomfort of his friends.

"I will send for you, so be ready on Odin's day morning. Now you must summon the servants for me, for I must have a brief word with them." That night as we lay with only the tips of our noses unwillingly protruding from the blankets and furs piled upon us, Astra shook me awake. "Husband, do you think they put too much reliance on us? Before the pirates tried to attack us, I had only one confrontation; it was with a stable boy who got too free with his hands."

"I've wondered the same thing. My magic is mostly that of protection. I can only negate the efforts of others to cast or use spells in fixed places like graves. Perhaps I can protect individual people as well. Time alone will tell. My father could summon fire, enough to light up the sky at night or to start a blazing fire in the hearth. I can get only a spark, and I have to sweat to do it. But maybe with some work, I can do better."

The following day brought a change in the weather. Not sunlight, of course; that would be asking too much for the weather most common at this time of year is gloom. Yet there was a change; it was warmer. Astra said a layer of warm air mixed with much moisture was upon us, and such conditions stretched in all directions with no end in sight; even rain was possible. The winds were swirling without a fixed direction, so she anticipated similar conditions to remain for the next few days. While this didn't bring joy to my heart, I was glad for the rise in temperature.

We spent the morning walking around in front of the farmhouse. Staying inside without exercise made our legs start to cramp. Our son was bored, of course; he couldn't wait to return to the palace where he could be with others his age.

But in the afternoon, I began to feel like something was out of place. The feeling of unease began to grow to the point where I had to tell Astra about it. But she, too, had the same growing dread. Maybe it was the gloom of the Dane weather that was oppressing us. With such weather, it was hard to be either optimistic or cheerful. Perhaps the gloom of winter had finally worn down our spirits. That explanation was as good as any, yet when we walked again in the afternoon, we both found ourselves scanning the tree line across the fields. Before we went in for the night, I sent Astra ahead while I stayed to talk to the guards. They kept two on duty at all times while the other two slept or cooked in the barn with the horses, where they made a fire pit. It was not comfortable by any means, but they got by. I told them about the mounting anxiety that I felt in my mind. They appeared to take my apprehensions seriously and promised to spend the night in a sleepless vigil. A very damp vigil, I suspected, as I felt the first few bits of sleet strike my cheek. I pulled the hood of my cloak over my head and walked to the house. It was still early evening when we finished eating, which gave me an opportunity to think of any added measures that I might make. There were three doors to the house, a rear one in the center and a door on either end. One entry was ours, the other to where the servants were staying: a room much like this one but only smaller. All of the doors were thick with heavy bolts; I knew some powerful spells to keep doors closed, but with servants and guards around, I hesitated to use them. After much consideration, I decided to forgo the use of magic. It was too dangerous to use here and might draw unwanted attention, but as it turned out, we received attention anyway.

A few hours before dawn, I woke up in a restless sweat. I got up to piss in the pot in the corner of the room, after which I threw some wood on the fire. I knew from long experience that I wouldn't be able to get back to sleep, so I decided to get dressed and sit by the fire. I hardly sat down when I heard faint noises I couldn't identify. My ears weren't the only ones to perk up; Astra suddenly sat upright, looked around, and asked what was going on. Flosi, too, woke when he heard us talking; his hearing was particularly acute.

"There are wolves, father; I can hear them." He said quietly.

"Wolves have come," said Astra after a moment's concentration, "the kind with two feet; your sword, husband."

While the two of them hurried to dress by the light of the fire, I struggled to don my heavy fur cloak. I quickly stuffed a knife with a soft leather scabbard into my waistband, took my sword from the wall, and carefully crept out the door. As soon as I was gone, Astra put the heavy wooden bar into place.

The fading light of the setting moon was enough to reflect off the sword blade. For this reason, I didn't take my helmet or shield. Walking carefully with my sword held low, I rounded the rear corner of the house. I could see the reflection of the flames from the fire pit through the open barn doors. Then suddenly, I heard savage cries and the clash of steel. Moving forward cautiously, I peeked around the corner of the barn door only to quickly pull back as a man with an arrow in his chest staggered backward, almost hitting me. A glance at this soon-to-be corpse showed that he was not one of ours.

As suddenly as the clamor of steel started, it stopped. I stuck my head around the corner, and seeing a familiar face; I called out as I had no intention of getting an arrow in the gut or an axe between my ears due to mistaken identity. Soon I was inside the barn listening to what the guards had to say.

"My lord," said the oldest man in charge, "we kept a close watch on the fields between here and the river. It's the only way to travel at this time of the year. To get here from the coast or King Bjornson's court riding overland would take days if it could be done at all. There were four of them; we watched as they came across the fields. We built up the fire, left the door open a little, and deceived them into thinking we were all sleeping using blankets and piles of straw. Torvald and Finki hid in the loft while we stayed in the shadows against the wall. These fine fellows," he said, pointing to the men holding bows, "are the Jarl's men; he left them here the other day, good shots they are. This big fellow," he said as he kicked the body of a huge man now sprawled out in death with an arrow through his throat, "was the first to fall. His friend beside him didn't fare too well either; he got an arrow in his shoulder and another in his leg before Nils stuck him with his spear. You already met the one who left us so soon that we hardly got to know him. And this one," he said, turning around, "got a bad feeling in his head when I threw my axe at him." As he said this, I could see a big gash on the man's forehead with blood all over his face.

I could only marvel at our good fortune in fighting off an attack like this with no injuries. Our guards could count on a large reward for their clear thinking and skill. Before going back to share the news of this attack with Astra and Flosi, I warned them against searching the bodies for valuables. At the mention of poison blades found on the man apprehended at the palace, they recoiled in a very prudent fear. Daylight was approaching, so I told their leader they must send word to the nearby village telling what happened. Then I headed to the house to tell Astra and Flosi what had transpired. Of course, they were elated at the news, surprised too that none of our people were hurt, for they knew enough of the world to understand that even successful conflicts involving swords, axes, and spears usually end in death, wounds, and maiming to both sides. Seldom does one side completely evade the butcher's bill.

The sun had yet to climb very high when the village headman and his sons arrived. He helped me inspect the bodies in the barn while his sons joined our guards in scouring the nearby countryside for any other unsavory characters that could be skulking about.

We examined the three average-sized men first; they were dressed very much alike. If fact, they looked enough alike to have been kin, perhaps. Nothing could be judged from the clothing or footwear, however. Only ordinary knives and small denomination common coins could be found on their persons. The amulets around their necks could be found on half the people on the island. But on their left shoulders was the small and sinister brand I had recently become aware of.

"These were pirates, to be sure," said the headman as he peered at the shoulder markings, "only pirates wear brands on their shoulders like these, not just any pirate either. My father was a sailor; he was born a Frisian and sailed the salt sea for most of his life; he told me never to trust a man with a brand on his shoulder because they're members of a secret order. The Angles drove them out years ago; where they are now, I couldn't say. But they're good people to stay away from. You're fortunate," he said, pausing to spit sideways, "they didn't expect you to have so many guards out here in the countryside; otherwise, they would have sent a whole ship's crew."

The big dead man wore neither armor nor an iron cap, but he did wear, under his cloak, layers of stiff boar hide probably boiled in wax. Many warriors wore this instead of expensive shirts of rings. He had a bag of silver pieces hidden under his outer clothes; a second bag was found, only this one was full of fine delicate beads of glass in different colors with tiny flakes of gold in them that sparkled in the light. Their great beauty, along with the precision of their casting, made them extremely attractive.

"He's different," said the old village headman looking down at him, "he's a berserker who fights for pay. See here," he said, pointing to multiple scars on his hands, forearms, face, and chest, "they don't feel pain when they get cut; the madness has them. It's very dangerous to be around them during a battle; a friend might get killed just as quickly as a foe."

"His eyes are blue; maybe he is from Scandia," I said as I tied a rope around his feet.

"You could be right," the old man said while rubbing his bristly chin, "that's where most of the berserkers come from. What will we do with his money and silver rings?" He asked as a horse dragged the man's body out.

"They go to the King, the beads too; mayhap we can find who made them."

"At any road, you can't stay here another night; it wouldn't be safe since your enemy knows where you are. There could be more of them about; it's best to head back to the palace. I'll get a sled for your things and horses for you to ride on. My sons will ride with you; you'll be safe enough returning to Roskilde."

"You're right," I said as I thought how glad my wife and son would be to find out that we're headed back to the palace, "I don't think that we'd have to worry about a berserker like that back at the palace; he'd be noticed. Let me go and help pack our clothes; I would very much like to reach the palace before dusk."

*

While Arn walked back to the house, another man of magic wended his steps to the artisan part of Roskilde, intent on buying a new and more comfortable chair for his quarters. Such was the tale that he told his servants. His true purpose in walking forth that day remains unknown.

As the day was partially sunny, a fine day for a walk, he took his time pausing to look at various items for sale that ranged from ducks, calves, and pies to blankets and door hinges. Steinson was a prudent man who had, as a tavern keeper's son, learned much about human nature before he had grown his first whisker. Some called him *a man who believed in naught*, but he would have disagreed strongly with that appraisal. He had faith enough, just not in the things that other people did. Mostly he believed in himself and his luck. In his thirty-eight years, he had learned to value self-reliance and his private feelings about destiny above all things. Today he wore the most common clothing and, as usual, took no guards with him. Few outside the palace knew who he was; among those who trudged through the muddy streets shopping for plucked chickens or bread, he was just another face. He habitually watched his back; it was his nature to do so, and today was no exception. His physical senses were not the only asset that probed the sea of humanity about him. His magic sent tendrils of an essence that would quiver in his mind when someone of a malevolent spirit sought him.

He was almost through the market when the hairs on the back of his neck began to bother him, as did a buzzing in his ears. He picked up his pace a bit, yet the feeling persisted; he was being followed. That realization put a chill through his liver as he paused to look at some freshly caught eels and crabs. He looked behind him while pretending to examine the fare being offered. Yet there was little to choose from in the mix of people he saw. All that he could see were people selling wares or women with market baskets. Added together, they wouldn't equal one good assassin. Even though he didn't see anyone following him, he picked up his pace, for by now, he knew that he was being stalked. He started casting his eyes around as he walked, looking for off-duty soldiers or young bravos that he could hire as bodyguards. He was handy enough with a knife to throw and stab, but he also knew that the Gods of combat were fickle. Sometimes even the best of warriors become food for the carrion birds. Then taking a quick look behind him to his left, he saw him; a tall, thin, sallow-visaged man with a dirty gray beard and lank locks falling out of a knit cap. He didn't try to hide his interest in Steinson; he merely curled his lip in a sneer when he was spotted.Steinson broke into a dead run entering the artisan part of the town heedless of the confusion he caused by knocking people down who he couldn't push out of the way. A quick look behind him showed the man chasing him only a few paces behind him. Too late, he saw the spear lowered in front of him; the point punched a hole in him just below his ribs; he was struck so hard that the spear stuck out of his back. After a quick realization that he had been herded like an animal into a trap, his eyes rolled back into his head, and he breathed no more. He heard none of the screams and yells that followed his death, for he was already on his way to whichever of the nine worlds would now be his home.

Our first intuition that something was wrong was at the rear gate of the city. Here the guards, seldom friendly, were more surly and suspicious than usual. We were kept waiting until a guard captain appeared. He recognized me, and after asking a few questions about the headman's sons, he let us enter. Obviously, something was wrong, but this man was not one to seek information from. The sun was now low in the sky as we rode through the mix of snow, ice, and mud. No doubt our faces would be well splattered by the time that we got to the palace.

When we arrived at the rear of the building, we could see small groups of people talking to each other. The servants who came out to take our baggage were plainly nervous and quiet. Experience told me that this was a bad omen; so were the many pairs of eyes that suddenly found the ground so interesting. We had hardly got through the door when I was accosted by a guard who informed me that I was to accompany him to see Bormo, master of the household staff, and of course, the King's spies, while a servant escorted Astra and Flosi back to their quarters.

We walked to a part of the palace I'd never been to. It was in the portion of the building two stories high, which was still somewhat of a novelty among the Danes. He lived in the rear part of the building, the area above and behind the great hall. Apparently, the Danes had not yet learned how to calculate the proper cutting of stairs, for these steps were all slightly different heights, nor were they completely level. There would be no question, though, of some killer being able to sneak in at night by stealth; every step squeaked or squawked when stepped on, some loudly.

The guard gave several low raps on the door, which caused a small window to be opened. A pair of eyes looked us over, some voices were heard, and then we could hear a heavy bar being moved out of the way and a metal bolt being slid. The door opened to see a plump round face of a servant dressed in the standard red and black worn by the servants to the court's inner circle.

After giving my cloak to a second servant, I was escorted to a small anteroom to wash my travel-stained face and dirty hands. Also, to take a much-needed piss into a rather ornate chamber pot. Looking less like an offering to the God of Dirt, I was escorted to the table of Bormo, who, despite his high position, scorned the use of any other name.

He rose at my coming and motioned me to a chair as servants hastened to bring me food and drink.

"Sad business," said the man across from me as he ripped a chicken carcass apart, not the first one either, judging from the pile of bones just taken away by a servant, "his death will be mourned. We will mourn his death and then avenge it; I will supervise the torment of the responsible ones. Have you not heard? I suppose they were too afraid to tell you. Steinson was assassinated this morning in broad daylight; they say he was going to buy a new chair."

This unwelcome news almost drove me to the floor. I had always thought him too crafty to be killed by such means. Maybe it worked because he never expected to be attacked in the open like this. My appetite left me, so I pushed the food away and reached for the wine.

"Eat, my friend, eat," said the big man softly, "we have much work to do, and you will need all of your strength. Tomorrow night we will burn his body in the courtyard. The King will have words to say." He then began to relate the details of the runemaster's death, as much as was known. After hearing the sad details about my friend's death, I told him about my own escape the previous night.

"It is my understanding that the money found on criminals belongs to the King, according to the laws of the Danes, so I've been told," I said as I took the bag from my belt that contained the coins and silver rings of the berserker and placed it on the table, "here too are some glass beads found on him; beads that took much skill to make."

"You are right, Master Arn; there are only a few, a very few, who have the skill to make these. The money I will give to Nakdan, but these beads, I will keep myself for now." Saying this, he held one bead up to the light studying it intently. He put them back in the bag and gave them to a servant to put away. Fresh seedcakes were brought when the chicken was cleared from the table. The death of Steinson had robbed me of my appetite, but the cakes smelled too good to ignore, so I nibbled on one of them as we sat and talked.

"So, the berserker had money but no brand; the three others had brands but no money. Then there are those curious beads. The day following an attempt on your life, our friend, who was also a master of runes, was murdered in the street. Beyond that, a jarl of Jutland has sent an emissary to the King concerning the Fang Islands pirates who, he says, plot against us. As you know, most Jutes live on the finger of land that sticks out into the sea like Odin's cock, although some have emigrated to southern Britain. The Fang Islands are on the far side of Jutland, along the coast. In the past, it was deserted except for a few sheepherders, but now it has become a den of raiders and pirates. They have raided the Franks and the Frisians, even sailing down the rivers of old Gaul to attack cities. When that tired them, they raided Less Britain and the coastal islands near where Saxon King Redwald now holds sway over much of the land. They are very energetic," he said as he reached for another cake, "they have also been to Scandia. Apparently, they do not fear the necromancer that is whispered about so much."

"We don't know if there is such a person," I said as I reached for more wine. The day's news left me with little appetite for food, yet I felt a rising desire for a strong drink.

"I think there must be something evil going on up there. I'll tell you something, something that I learned long ago. Always assume the worst when you have a situation where the facts are disputed or unknown; if you do that, you will seldom be disappointed. We must also keep an open mind; problems seldom come singly; no, they often bring others with them."

"Did Steinson have any ideas about what was going on? I always had the feeling that he knew more than he said." I said as I put my glass down, suddenly feeling tired.

"He was not a man to share his thoughts until he was forced to do so by circumstances," the heavy man said as he twirled his mustache end with his hand, "he was good at keeping secrets. Yet he came to me on Freya's day last and asked me to keep a watch on a house in the artisan section. The man who lives and works there," he said significantly, "made things from glass, even fancy beads."

I was exhausted and heavy at heart at the news of Steinson's death. As I rose, Bormo grabbed my arm while giving me a hard look.

"There is one more thing. The cook, who we think was the one who tried to poison you, was found not long after Steinson was murdered. He was in a ditch, half-buried in filth not far from here. I think he was killed soon after he escaped from the palace kitchen. He was not robbed; he had silver coins hidden in his clothing. His neck was sliced so deeply that his head was nearly cut off. Whoever did it wanted to be very sure he was dead. I looked at the body; he, too, had the mark you and Steinson discussed. What it means I do not know yet it is clear that a conspiracy exists."

With these words, we ended our evening parley, the news of the day so addled my thinking that I scarcely noticed the guard who walked behind me as I made for our quarters. When I reached our lodging, the servant outside the hall rose and quickly knocked on the door. This was opened by another servant helping to put food on the table. The fare was hot bread, pottage, mutton stew, and chicken. But I could tell that my wife and boy had also lost their appetites, for both had red-tinged eyes. Although Steinson was not family, he was a man we saw every day for months, save for the time we spent on that frozen farm. There was little that I could say in the way of comforting words. The world is a brutal place; we never know who will be next. All I could do was hold them tight and tell them a little about what Bormo had told me. A short while later, I called a servant and had her clear the table of food. We then lay in a real bed for a welcome change, yet the night felt sullen and cheerless. Strange sounds haunted my dreams that night; I heard a horn in the distance, crows flying overhead, and the cadence of oars being raised. There was little cheer the next day, for Steinson's death had cast a pall over everyone. No doubt, word of the attack on my family had quickly spread.

The great bell sounded in the early evening, summoning everyone to the courtyard to say goodbye to the former Master of Runes. Torches and braziers were lit in the courtyard to give light and to show the high status of the man who now lay on a lofty wooden pyre. Women had been hired to wail and cry; they certainly earned their money with loud lamentations and tearful appeals to the Gods. There were at least 200 people there, not counting the guards. All were armed, myself included, for to honor the fallen, iron must be worn.

The rites began when the King arrived with his court and family members. A black bull, young and without blemish, was led forward to the waiting priest, who sang a tuneless dirge before cutting its throat. With a thud, it fell to the courtyard paving stones. The priest's assistants quickly took a shallow bowl to catch the bull's blood as the animal kicked feebly. This blood was smeared on the face of Steinson's corpse.

"Just be glad we're not living in Rus," I whispered to Astra as she turned her head away, "they would have cut the throats of a couple of slave girls too."

At this point, the King holding his wife's hand, stepped in front of the brier and spoke about how he admired Steinson's dedication as a member of the palace household and praised him for his courage, steadfastness, and skill. When he spoke of the nameless assassins that killed his loyal servant, I saw color rising on the King's face. He commanded that all who knew anything about this murder come forward immediately or face an unpleasant death. Whoever would give the names of those responsible would be rewarded with their weight in fine silver. Then, after the priest chanted a final prayer to the Gods and poured oil on the body, the King grabbed a torch and lit the pyre. As the fire leaped from log to log, I could only stand there and wonder at the turn my life had taken in the last year. I went from a craftsman and farmer who dabbled in magic to standing near a King as the body of a friend was being turned into ashes. Astra sobbed as she stood next to me; being a woman, she was free to cry all she wanted, which was denied to me. I could see Flosi fighting back the tears too. Steinson was not a man who was easy to warm up to, yet I noticed that not all of the women who sobbed loudly were paid to do so. After the fire had burned for a while, the King entered the great hall where the banquet was being served; people drifted away.

"We should go home, as I told you before; this is no place for us. Next time you'll be the one with a spear in your belly. I don't know who is behind this, but whoever it is must be powerful. Flosi isn't safe here either." Astra said while looking earnestly into my eyes.

"We have about as much chance at being allowed to return home as me riding yonder hairy star," I said, glancing up at the heavens. "The king lost his Master of Runes. So, where do you think that leaves us? To say nothing about your own abilities. No, my dear, I don't think either of us will see home for quite some time."

Astra reacted with a look of resignation. The reality of our situation was not of our choosing, yet complaining about the will of the Gods was pointless. She understood this as much as I did.

The smell of cooked meat was overwhelming when we entered the hall; the tables were packed, and everyone who was anyone was in attendance. It was expected that everyone pay homage to the memory of a fallen hero. If Steinson was not precisely a hero, he was close enough not to matter.

After everyone had eaten and drank enough to take the edge off their appetite, Jarl Hakon rose to give a speech. On such occasions, people expected much in the way of speeches. I recognized it as the type of talk jarls and other public men had ready for such events, only changing the details to suit the circumstances. He talked of honor and dignity, of fealty, and the importance of oath-keeping. He also spoke of the Gods who expect certain types of conduct from men. He ended by putting his lips to his cup in fond remembrance of his friend. Before he resumed his seat, he called on everyone to remain quiet while the King spoke.

"My friends," the King boomed, "we have sent the spirit of our servant and friend onward to dwell wherever the Gods choose to send him. It is true that he was not a man for combat with a sword or axe, yet he was a warrior. He had other weapons to use against our enemies. It is my hope that he is given a seat in the great hall of Odin even if he must enter by the back door in the middle of the night." This brought out a few muted laughs from those who knew Steinson and his lack of scruples when it came to getting what he wanted. "But now we must deal with the future. We must protect ourselves from those who practice the dark arts; we need a man who can resist the enchantments of Black Magic. Fortunately, we don't have far to look; there is one here tonight who has the power to defeat such evil. We have a man whose grandfather defeated the King of the Dead. Then split his head open with his axe for good measure. The father of the man I speak was employed by powerful warlords, even among the Rus. I don't need to tell you how hard-headed those people can be. Come forward, Master Arn and take your oath; come forward, pledge yourself, and share in the riches that come to those who do their duty."

I got up from the bench with the feeling of the utmost dread. I found it a severe challenge to my abilities to present the calm exterior that would be expected on such an occasion. Doubtless, there were some fools present who looked upon me with envy. I felt like the man who wanted to show some composure when he was taken to be hung by saying: "If it weren't for the honor of this, I would gladly trade places with somebody else."

When I stood before the King, I bowed and drew my sword from its scabbard. Then I held my sword across my hands, knelt, and recited the pledge: "I swear to protect the King and his family from all dangers. I give this oath willingly. Let the Gods punish me forever if I should fail in my duty; this I swear." Following the oath, the King stood, as did everyone else; he thrust forward his right hand so I could kiss his arm ring. He took from the table a silver band, placed it on my wrist, raised my arm, and called out, **Hail, Master Arn**. The people in the room answered him with loud cries of approval; others chanted; some pounded their mugs on the table while others clapped. The call of *Arn*, *Arn*, and *Arn* echoed throughout the room. During the uproar, I saw, much to my horror, the rune-covered coat of Steinson and his hated hat being brought to me. With great ceremony and clamor, these habiliments were put on me. When the black ribbons were tied under my chin, there was naught that I could do but smile and bow to the enthusiastic crowd. My helpless gaze fell upon my wife, who stood there feebly clapping her hands, with eyes as large as warming pans at the sight of such a peculiar apparition; as for Flosi, he cheered lustily.

Chapter Four
Dead Men Talk & The Sinister Brand

I now found my life full of toil and bother; as an official of the court, I was bound to attend all the meetings and shoulder my part of the duties. Much of this was done in concert with Bormo, whose spies we depended on; at the moment, they had plenty to do. This included watching two places merited attention. The first of these was the one who made fine things from glass, according to the spymaster. The other one being watched was also somehow suspicious; in what way, I wasn't told. Master Bormo often met with me; we spoke long and hard about the information from spies and the gossip heard in the taverns and brothels. Some information he paid silver for, and some information came from those whom he had a hold over; still, others reported in the hope that if they were involved in future trouble, their contributions would help them. Yet, for all of this, we did not know where the lair of this cancerous growth might be. We knew that hostile forces were gathering but not who was behind it or where they would strike first.

It was the start of Harpa, the month of the daughters, after which came the month of Skorpla, which marked the beginning of the raiding season. I, too, began a quest for information; I thought it prudent to learn more about the country that I was now a high official of. While the opinions of the high and mighty were there for the asking, I decided to see how things were looked at by those who did the lifting, the hauling, the growing, and the shoveling. To that end, I started to visit the taverns where I met a variety of people; some were merchants who told me what was in demand and what was not, while tradesmen and artisans talked of their work and groused about their problems. Most of all, I met sailors who liked to drink, talk, and gamble, especially with me, for I have always had a poor hand at throwing dice. I often spoke to those who had sailed west, who knew the coast and ports of the Franks and the Jutes, everywhere else west of Kattegat. Most of whom had also sailed to Scandia at one time or another. I learned many things from these men; I came to understand the types of craft and how they would fare in a storm. Also, what Gods they worshiped and their methods of divination for sailors are much given to the words of fortune tellers and the observers of signs. Yet most of their talk followed the markets, the cost of cloth, iron, leather, hides, and metal pots; always, the lure of money had to be weighed against the risks. Information was constantly sought by those who sail the sea, so my questions didn't seem suspicious or out of place. I prided myself on my ability to mix well with men of different classes and occupations; now, I had full scope to practice this art.

The next quarter-moon, I met Bormo in a tavern; he had sent for me to come in haste. He disliked mixing with those below his station, despite his humble beginning. He obviously regarded himself as a superior member of society, far above the common herd. He wore the best clothing, silks imported from far away, even past the land of the Rus. He also loved shirts with lace only made in Flanders, his furs from the far north of Scandia. Yet tonight, when we met at the Inn of the Two Anchors, he wore the leathers of a man at arms covered with a dark hood. That fact alone told me that there was serious work to be done.

"Tell me again how this happened," I asked.

"There is little to tell. Our man was watching the glass worker's shop from across the way when he heard a noise; he saw a man stumble out the door with a knife sticking out of his belly. Who this man is, we have no idea; he had never been there before. My men are now asking who he belongs to, but I think he was a merchant. Our spy got a horse and rode right away to see me, so I took a few guards and went to investigate. We entered the house and found nobody; the man we watched must have escaped during the commotion. We have his description: he is short, pot-bellied with a straggly black and grey beard; he walks with a sullen, downcast look about him."

"Master Bormo, you have just described half the men of this city. Is that the best that you can do?"

"By the All-Father, you are not such a dull man after all," he said laughing, "the only other thing is that he is said to be missing his small finger on his left hand. Of course, we want to see if he has anything on his shoulder."

Bormo took me to a shed close behind the barracks; I recognized a few of his people lounging outside. They were a hard-bitten lot who scarcely noticed me. As we approached the building, a tall man came out the door, wiping blood off his hands with a rag.

Bormo, master of spies and assassins

"What's new, Gautyre?" Bormo asked as the man stood in front of us.

"He died a short time ago; he wailed and begged the Gods for mercy but told us nothing, not even his name."

"Come, my friend," I whispered to Bormo, "let us see what we can see."

Then we walked through the usual low Dane door into a room lit only by an oil lamp. On a table lay the victim's body, his face already beginning to turn grey. He was well dressed, not richly, but he wore clothing and boots of quality. He was not young; there were grey streaks in the brown hair of his head and beard, and he wore a few cheap amulets on a chain around his neck. At the base of his throat, just visible under his beard, was a large festering boil. As I looked the man over, Bormo finished cutting his clothing off; on his left shoulder, we found what we were looking for; the Christian symbol inverted. He was killed on the premises of a glass worker, who now fled, one so skilled that he was one of the very few in the north capable of making colorful gold-flecked beads found on the body of the berserker assassin.

"Do you have any ideas about why this man died?"

"No," replied Bormo as we walked towards the palace, "but the man was up to something; the mark on his shoulder tells us that. It has been my experience that violence is frequent among thieves and plotters. They have no honor, so it is easy for them to kill each other."

"Will you catch this glass maker?" I asked.

"We might if he is still alive, but he might be dead too, for all I know. There is another man, one who might be connected to this fellow. We'll see what goes on with him; we noticed a number of people going directly from the glass maker's shop to this fellow's forge. Maybe it's a coincidence; whatever it is, I will keep you informed. The goings-on there, or more precisely, the lack of such, caused us to scratch our heads. Nobody called after dark, Bormo's spies said, not even a whore or a smuggler, nor even friends to play dice with or drink wine with the smith. Spies posing as customers came out shrugging their shoulders. He was good at his craft but had a bad reputation as being ill-natured. Bormo was deeply suspicious of a man who didn't gamble or go to taverns or see whores; such a man had something to hide.

Reports came in daily as merchants and passing travelers were more numerous now that the weather was improving. Some of their stories caused us great anxiety. So alarmed was I that in the mornings I went, with Astra and Flosi, to the barracks yard for practice in combat. We trained with all sorts of weapons, even with staves and throwing knives.

Word now freely circulated that the King would go north into Scandia with great strength as soon as the weather warmed enough. As members of the household, we were given ring shirts and helmets at the King's expense. Astra's ring shirt and leathers caused quite a stir among the capital's inhabitants when she wore them to the practice yard. Shieldmaidens were often mentioned in stories but seldom seen in real life. I admit to teasing her, saying how attractive she looked in such garb, one night as I sat back in the comfortable bed that had formerly been owned by my predecessor, I had inherited his quarters along with his possessions, my mind turned to the lengthy conversation that I had that morning with a farmer who had fled Scandia. He owned his land, which singled him out as a man of substance; farmland was scarce in a place mainly consisting of bare rock, forests, and mountains. It would take a lot to force a man like this from his farm. He related tales of resurrected people coming in hordes to rend the bodies of the living. They were joined by trolls and other beasts with huge mouths crammed with long yellow fangs stained with blood. Above, strange birds swooped down to peck the eyes out of the harried villagers as they fled along the road. Row upon row of the dead marched forward with rotted, unseeing eyes leaving a field of ruin and destruction. It was almost beyond belief that something like this could occur, yet as I probed the man's mind, I could detect no lies or deception. He believed what he saw, and what he saw was something not to be seen until the final battle; these revelations haunted me for some time.

A few nights after I had heard this frightening tale, I was in bed, exhausted by the press of work, while waiting for Astra to finish washing and join me when I found my eyes too heavy to keep open. When I did open them, I found myself far outside our rooms in the palace, drifting far away from Roskilde.

I was seated at a table under a tree watching as a serving woman in a brilliant white apron poured me a glass of mead. Across from me sat a broad-shouldered man with long blonde hair streaked with grey; his double-braided beard was the same color. He was occupied at the moment in spreading honey on his bread. On his forearms was the ink art of dragons mixed with the symbols of runes and magic; on his arms were silver bands of rank. Behind him was a bay full of trading ships and seagulls that flew noisily overhead.

"You are back, my young pup; you must have encountered more difficulties. That is not to be wondered at considering your current lofty condition." Here he indulged himself in a fit of laughter.

"Yes, grandfather, it appears that I have once again decided to consult you."

"That is not surprising considering the mess you made when you questioned that farmer from the long fjord in Scandia. You might as well have turned the matter over to your son; he could have done as well."

"The stories told by the farmer were a caution. The images were of unrestrained blood lust; a harvest of horror, dead men by the thousands marching towards us."

"Have we reached the final day when such things can expect to be seen? Is the All-father marshaling his forces to lead out of Asgard?"

"No, grandfather, it is not the last day. Heimdahl has not blown the warning, nor have the Gods assembled."

"That should tell you all you need to know. But enough of the marching dead; tell me what else goes on."

"There are the usual quarrels among jarls over land. The Saxon King in south Albion grows richer and stronger; there is also the matter of the Fang Islands. They raid everywhere; it is said that they seek a new home. Getting information about them is always difficult; those who meet them don't usually survive."

"I sincerely hope you don't have those people to deal with. They have the perfect place for their base," the old man said as he took an apple from the table, "the shifting sand of their islands protects them. The channels can change after a single storm. They have grown monstrously rich over the years, yet they grow only a little grain. At best, their lands are fit only for pasture and not much of that. So, what are they to do? Gold is a wonderful thing, but you can't eat it. Most of what they eat is brought in by ship, but what if the ships are lost in a storm or defeated in battle?"

"Then they would starve," I replied.

"Yes, my good Arn, they would starve. What do you think they do all winter when the sea is too rough and cold to sail in? Do they only huddle before the fire listening to old women tell tales?"

"They probably do listen to stories, but that's not all that they would do, grandfather; I expect they would try and come up with a solution to their problem. They would scheme, and they would plot. Who would be weak enough for them to conquer? Where would be their best chance?"

"It seems that you have at least learned the basic facts about the times we live in. Plotting is what men do, so the enemies with imagination are the most dangerous. The Fang Islanders have a long and complicated history; wherever they have lived, they have either conquered their difficulties or moved on to greener pastures. So far, their neighbors have not been roused to gather their strength and attempt to stamp them out, but if goaded, they will try it. What would you do if you were in their place?"

"The adages all say, grandfather, that when strength alone won't do, then craft and guile are required, stratagems must be employed."

"Very good, my lad, very good. But I would amend that to say that in *ALL* circumstances, first use your head and your imagination before you expend the blood of your young men."

"They might well hire a person with powers. Such people are rare, grandfather, yet you were one of them."

"True enough, you must remember your father; he had power also and a fine mind. Your own powers are considerable, as are those of your wife. Yet such power is not confined to one family. Others have found it before us; those who follow us will also find it. The man who filled that bay with corpses years ago had power, too; it took much to do that."

"His assistant has never been found nor his books; now comes a threat from the north. Certainly, one with magic and evil mixed together."

"Just so, my lad, just so," he said as he sipped his drink, "there is a famous saying from a dead Emperor in a region far to the south, 'For everything ask *what its nature and substance is, the reason for being?*' That is a question that you must always ask. Train hard with your body but exert your thinking even more. Sit on the cold and wet throne of the Fangs and ask what can be done for your family and people. Take your mind over Scandia like a bird; what is the nature of the lands below you? Never stop asking questions. Don't wait for the battle to approach, my boy, don't sit there like a frog on a tree stump; no, use your mind with the disciplines of power that your father taught you. Call out the runes by name, arrange them, and wake them up from their slumber. If you wait for the battle to approach, it will be too late. Use the red-bellied hellebore root when you feel strong enough; think about this, and you'll know what to do. And now, my boy, it's time for my afternoon nap, so you must go home."

I awoke in the morning feeling tolerably refreshed but with a daunting task to accomplish. The challenge my grandfather proposed to me was severe but needed if I could ever exert myself as a Runemaster fully, yet this was not a step to be taken lightly. On the way past the table, I grabbed a hunk of bread left from the night before and a skin of wine. I also stopped to retrieve a couple of small roots from my leather pouch of herbs I had brought here from the village. I left word with a servant for my wife and son not to look for me at the training yard this morning as I had other things to do.

The first warming rays of the sun were striking the harbor as I walked past the docks. A few minutes later, I was cutting through the boat yard; men were arriving for their daily labor; a few gave me curious looks as I wended my way through the ships in varying stages of construction or repair.

At length, I came to the north tower, which is located on the extreme northwestern edge of the city's defenses, located in the corner of the harbor and curtain walls, making it the farthest from the palace; it needed to be strong; this indeed it was. The solid stone fortress was constructed to house up to a hundred men if required, but in times of peace, only a handful of men were stationed there. This was not my first visit here by any means; it was a good place to hide when I wanted to be alone without fear of interruption. The commander, Boltar, a tough and taciturn Dane, seemed to understand my need for solitude. He gave me leave to go to the roof of the tower any time I chose to. Seeing the harbor from fifty feet in the air was worth seeing. Today was not a day for seeing the sights, though; I had a task to do. My grandfather's words from the night's dream echoed in my ears; I must concentrate on making my mind strong, very strong. With a quick word to the guard, I was let in; then, up the dank stone steps I went until I reached the ladder that led to the roof hatch, then out into stiff and rather cold morning breezes. I got a clear view of the harbor, the shipyard, the palace, and the vast tidal flats that extended north beyond the wall. With my back against the parapet wall, I sat in the sunlight, eating the bread and drinking the wine laced with the Black Drink I had brought; it's important to eat before chewing the sacred plant roots to avoid vomiting. By themselves, these roots were just tasteless fiber, but after chanting the hidden verses of power, they produced a powerful tonic that could allow a gifted one to see wide and far, uncover secrets, sharpen senses, and more. My father had told me that the God of the ancients, Janus, a God with one face looking forward and another looking behind, could be summoned by chewing these roots. He didn't sound enthusiastic about it, I recalled. Some people died from its use; others had gone mad, but to one like me who hungered for the power of sight, the risk would be taken. I put small pieces of root into my mouth and chewed; the taste was bitter. With a sing-song voice, I recited verses from the lore passed on to me; the chanting became increasingly difficult the more words I repeated, for the magic doesn't like to give up its secrets easily. I struggled with words that I had to drag out of my mouth by main force. When done, I was sweating and breathing hard; temporarily winded, I laid back and let the sun soak into my joints. I don't know how long I lay there like a log floating in a swamp, but I came to my senses at some point. Then I noticed a couple of gull feathers near my hand. Gull feathers are common enough by the ocean, but for some reason, they seemed important, so I leaned over and grabbed them.

 I sat there fascinated by the feathers like a boy who had seen them for the first time, wondering what it would be like to fly above our petty problems, to revel in the sunlight now flowing down upon me. For the first time in months, I felt warm and exhilarated, intoxicated even, with the feelings of air, light, and a soaring sensation as wings of spirit and thought carried me ever higher. I felt like one of the Gods racing across the sky. The clean and clear breezes of the heavens sustained me for a while. Then the winds faltered; my confidence was replaced by doubt. The heavens had closed their doors to me; from a great height, I started to fall.

 Terrified, I attempted to call out, but all I could mouth were squawks and inane ravings. Even those failed me as I felt my tongue grow leaden with my mouth full of ashes. Then the falling stopped, and

I was back again, leaning against the parapet. I could tell I was leaking liquid fire; I felt it scorching my hand. With difficulty, I moved my head so I could peer down at my left side; my hand was covered in blood, and in my right hand, I held my short knife; I had cut each finger, long, deep cuts from which the red fire freely flowed, the feathers were soaked in blood. Now I comprehend what had happened; I had achieved the gift of flight-sight; I could use the eyes of a bird to see. This power was now forever with me; I could transfer my sight and thought into a bird while my body remained inert. With practice, I could see for miles beyond what my human eyes could as I soared far into the sky.

I wasn't done, though; I had only opened the door to summon the ancient magic. This was a serious matter; I had gained a great gift. Would I be strong enough to keep it? This magic could be called by just about anyone who knew how to do it, even those who were unpracticed in these arts. Calling it is the easy part; surviving it is not. There was no guarantee that even an adept could control it and not be left as an empty, burned-out shell of what once was a human being. Now came the wild magic I had summoned, taking a hideous and grotesque shape. My ears rang as I heard it approach, ready to test me. I instinctively knew there could be only one winner; it would kill me, or I would survive to make it my servant; there was no middle ground. A battle was about to be joined; not one fought with shield and spear; no, a struggle within my mind for mastery. Just as the one who dwelt in Frigg's embrace paid for knowledge with his eye, spells, too, must be earned.

It came to my mind as a wolf-like creature from the darkest reaches of my imagination. I saw an obscenely long tongue hanging from its diseased jaws as it lurched forward. Its claws scratched along the stones with a sound that made my flesh crawl, its eyes burning with an unnatural green fire. I didn't bother to reach for my dagger; no weapons of steel could kill such a beast. So loathsome was it that it would have never been allowed to disgrace the streets of Hel. Reaching forward with my hand, I began to trace out the words that the fates first spoke to Odin as he hung from the tree of life impaled by his own spear, a sacrifice to himself by himself. As I traced the runes in the air, they began to glow.

It was after dark when they found me. Search parties had been out for hours by the time somebody bothered to ask at the north tower for word of me. Even then, they weren't sure, but since nobody could remember seeing me leave, they made haste to check the roof. I was roused into consciousness, but I could not immediately explain the burn marks on my clothing, the hair pulled out of my head, or my blood-soaked hands. With the help of strong men, I was lowered down the ladder into waiting arms and then carried to a cart in the front. Needless to say, everyone from the lowest servant to my wife and son made a lot of unnecessary noise upon my safe arrival back at the palace. My various wounds made them think that I was the victim of an attempted murder; no explanation to the contrary seemed to satisfy anyone. Astra claimed that she never believed for an instant that I was dead, yet she covered her mouth when she saw my condition. I was marked all over with bruises, cuts, and burns. The fleshy part of my calf even had bite marks on it.

I kept to my bed for the next few days, not that I lacked company. One of the visitors was the King, who talked privately with me for a long time. Astra was mystified that the King, famous for his brevity of speech, impatience, and restless nature, could sit still that long. I told her that she did the King wrong, that he did indeed have the ability to concentrate, especially if his self-preservation was at stake.

I healed rapidly, which didn't surprise me as I now felt twice the man I was just a week ago. It was well that I had recovered from my inner struggle as quickly as I did, for two days later, Astra awakened me in the middle of the night. Outside, one of Bormo's men stood with a small squad of soldiers holding a lantern. I quickly dressed and followed them outside the harbor wall to a small fish house on the waterfront. Inside I found Bormo wrapped in a long dark cloak against the night chill, sitting on a bench, twisting the ends of his mustache; on a table in the center of the room was the body of a man. By the feeble light of a couple of rush and tallow lamps, I could see that he was an undistinguished-looking man of middling age. His squat face, spare beard, and lank hair were as common as the dirt that he had under his fingernails. Around his neck was a tightly knotted rope that had been used to kill him.

"He was found by the watch being loaded into a boat. Three or more men were involved, but they ran off as soon as they were discovered. The body is fresh, not stiff even now." He said as he got up, walked over to the corpse, and picked up the dead man's hand.

"This can only be the glass worker; you wouldn't have gotten me out of bed for an ordinary murder."

"Right you are; I wanted to have you here before he is searched." With this said, he began to cut away the man's clothing. He wore a common brown tunic that reached his knees and belted at the waist. Around his legs, he wore hose that tied just above the knee; his shoes were of goatskin cut in the Saxon manner and were wrapped in an old coat full of moth holes. We found the brand, as expected, on his left shoulder. Nothing else could be found on him; he had been stripped of everything.

"These people, whoever they are, leave no living men to tell tales. I suppose we can leave now. I wanted you here so there would be no questions later about the body. He'll be food for the fish and crabs, I think; unless they are burning trash today, then they might burn him."

"Hold," I said as I stood there thinking. "Perhaps it is not just the living who can tell a tale. Maybe this bird will sing a song for us. He who is glad of war used spells to talk to the dead; one of those spells is known to me." Bormo's eyes opened wide at this. Paying him no further notice, I gathered my powers and ordered my mental forces. Attempting this was reckless, but my grandfather's prodding and my use of the red hellebore root had made me bold.

"**Manaz** makes me see, **Gebo** calls my friends, **Fethu** brings a goat, **Othela** hides from me, **Uruz** rides an ox, **Perth** sings a song, **Nathus** sharpens a sword, **Ingas** is a mother "

I recited the names of the runes in the simple chanting rhyme that I learned as a boy. As I sounded their names, the runes appeared before me, hanging in the air, all burning with colored flames. The air now reeked with the smell of sulfur and pitch. Once I had them all in front of me, pulsing with fire, I closed my eyes; in my mind's eye, I pictured several words that I stitched together to make a verse. Then I forced myself to chant the spell:

Speak of ships, tell of tales, mouth your mother's name. Sing of iron, talk of maidens, weep for dole and pity. Near or far come to me. Show me what the Norns carved for you, only sleep when I release you.

At this, the runes disappeared. At once, the dead man's body trembled, and then his eyes opened; opened in terror. He worked his mouth, but no sounds came out that could reach our ears. Yet I understood his words in my mind; many questions I compelled him to answer, unwilling as he was, he could not refuse me. This was the first time I talked with a dead man outside of a dream. He stood in front of me, in my mind's eye anyway, a shade surrounded by fog. A swirling mist circled him in an uneasy dance; it was time to walk across the bridge into Hel. Angry at the delay, tendrils of smoke reached out to grab him, but all such attempts failed as I had him trapped like a fly on the end of a frog's tongue. The daughter of the trickster would have to wait until I was done with him; then, she could take him with good riddance. I saw images in his mind, fleeting at first but more substantial as I grew accustomed to the task. His knowledge was more limited than I had hoped for. His motivation was easy to understand; he wanted gold. He killed the merchant out of sheer, unthinking panic when the man tried to blackmail him over the death of Steinson. The merchant knew that he had hired the killer that waylaid the former runemaster. Indeed, I saw the face of the killer and where I might find him. I saw many other things, some questions were answered, but many were not; nonetheless, I gained some understanding of his life and purpose. It seemed like I talked to him for ages before letting him go, although Bormo told me it had been only a short time. "The next time you speak to spirits or dead men, please let me know in advance," he said as he wiped the sweat from his brow. "So, tell me, who is this man, and where did he come from?"

"He was a Frank. Years ago, he was an apprentice to a glass worker. He killed his master, took his money, and then went to the Saxons for a while. While there, he met criminals; he joined them but only after they had the mark put on his shoulder. He murdered somebody again, this time for pay. He called himself Grim Eberson, but that wasn't his real name; he didn't come here of his own accord; no, he was sent here. There was little to be learned from his mind; he did what he was told and kept his mouth shut. But you were right to be suspicious about the weapon maker. He is hiding the man who killed Steinson; I'll tell you where."

"Did you see who was behind the plot to assassinate Steinson?"

"He never knew who it was, for the man was heavily cloaked. He could have been an old man; that's all he knew. He paid the men who tried to kill me, and one of them stole from him the glass beads that you found. They came from Jutland, all of them."

"I don't understand one other thing; both men had the same shoulder mark, so they must have been part of the same conspiracy. But you tell me he tried to extort money from the glass artisan. How can that be?"

"There is no limit to the greed of men who hire themselves out. These are rootless oath-breakers who have no loyalty to jarl, king, or family. Where this man went wrong," I said as I turned and pointed to the corpse, "was that he panicked when threatened with exposure. The merchant couldn't have done this without betraying his own involvement. He should have laughed then booted the man out of his shop with a few kicks to his arse."

"It was his fate, no doubt," said Bormo as he made to leave the shack, "his fate, it turned out, was to our benefit. Come now, my strange friend who keeps magic under his hat; let us have something to eat; the sun is rising, and so is my appetite."

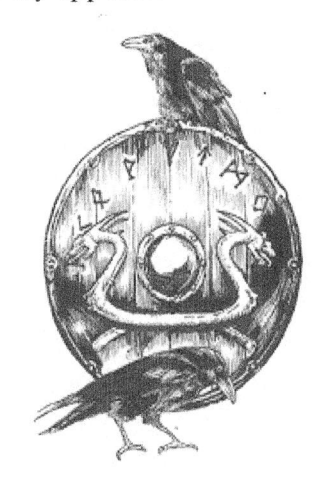

Chapter Five

The Neo-Necromancer

The next Tyr's day following the new moon.

Astra looked very appealing in her shirt of rings that covered a jerkin of supple black leather and leggings. She was standing in our palace abode eating bread from off the table. A wooden box containing her clothing stood near the door, waiting to be taken aboard the ship. I wonder if she realized the great favor that was allowed her as room aboard a ship of war was very limited. Only those of the highest rank would have been allowed to take up so much space with mere clothing.

I came up behind her, playfully grabbing her, but she smacked my hands away, claiming that she had thrice this week played the part of a Valkyrie raising a not-so-dead warrior for her bed. We needed to quicken our movements anyway as the auspices would be taken soon, and, if favorable, which I considered very likely, being the beginning of Skorpla, the start of the raiding season, we would set sail.

A short time later, with helm upon my head, my sword strap looped over my left shoulder, and clad in mail, I walked with Flosi and his mother out of the palace door, followed by servants carrying what baggage we chose to take with us. I eschewed the garb of Steinson; I felt every inch a warrior as I strode along, Astra struggling to keep pace. As I puffed my chest out in martial pomp and pride, I hoped I would not attract the plague of fleas that often set up residence under armor.

The harbor was overflowing with men, servants, slaves, horses, and a few criminals waiting to be sacrificed. Two of them were robbers who had killed their victims; a thoughtful jarl had brought them along as a gift. Added to this entertainment, two other men were to be whipped and castrated for the edification of the populace. They would not be killed, though, at least not right away. These two men were responsible for the death of Steinson; they would be tied to stakes in the slack tide to become food for the crabs as the water returned to the harbor. The populace would then be treated to the spectacle of the killers being munched on by the teeth and pincers of those who lived in the bay before drowning.

As close as we were to the festivities, our view was less than perfect, for we couldn't see the ritual sacrifice of the animals. There were just too many people in the way. Likewise, our view of the two vile oafs who had killed Steinson was minimal, yet we could hear them well enough. When the torments started, the men yelped in pain, much to the crowd's amusement; the executioner was later praised for using a dull knife to cut off parts of their anatomy. Although we didn't get a good view of the whippings and castrations, we had no problem seeing the other two criminals being executed. They were strung up high enough for all to get a good look at. The Danes put much store on how well men died; viewed in this light, these men earned no favors from the Almighty Beings. They yelled and cried, kicked their feet, and shit themselves, much to the disgust of everyone.

The time had come for the ships to be boarded, so I kissed my shield maiden wife on her mouth and both cheeks and bid the captain to take good care of her. To the absolute surprise of all but a few people, I gave her a final wave and headed for a ship at the rear of the line. Even my son didn't know what was going on. I told him that due to certain requirements, we had to split up; he thought this odd but accepted the explanation. My words to him were simple, don't disgrace yourself with bad conduct now that your parents are away, and above all things, obey the Queen who was nominally in charge of him. She, of course, was present for the sacrifices; no doubt she gave her husband an effusive farewell. Like everyone at court, she knew the value of correct public behavior and played her part well.

I walked down to the end of the docks, where I got into a dory, taking the tightly wrapped leather bags as the servants handed them to me. We headed for where Jarl Hakon Harefoot had his ships anchored in the harbor. I sat in the bow as the men rowed me to the *Ocean Bride*, the biggest of the Jarl's three ships. This is a new ship, although a little different from the King's warship; it was shorter but deeper with higher sides, built with bad weather in mind. While there were fewer men than on the King's ship, more supplies were stored on board. Between our three ships, we had over 100 men. They were picked men, though, the best of the best. As soon as I was on board, the ships lifted their anchors and ran their oars out. Our vessels were the last in line, so we had to wait our turn. In the meantime, the good Jarl served me fresh bread washed down by fine beer. I took full advantage of these things, for sea voyages made even common food like this look like luxuries later on.

The fleet made a stirring sight as it left the harbor unfurling its sails when they reached the open sea. There were some 17 ships besides ours. All were Danes; the King thought it best to let the soldiers of his allies till their fields for the time being. The start of a year's sailing season was always one of uncertainty. The jarls, high men, mostly wealthy landowners, and the like went into the winter with full barns meaning that they emerged from the enforced hibernation none the worse for wear, unlike other years when the people were eating tree bark by the time the snow melted. But how many remained loyal when the ice melted in the fjords and lakes? There were always those who were unhappy over disputes about property that went against them. Landless younger sons with little to lose were ready to listen to stories of wealth and fame that could be had by switching sides. What good, they reasoned, was a sworn oath if they were too poor to attract a respectable woman? A kept oath would not bring them new clothes in a world that judged so much by appearances. Why should they be forced to wear rags all because of the selfishness of the landowner? A Dane would become wild with anger if anyone were to suggest that he was a man who would break a solemn oath to his jarl or king, yet the Danes broke such vows repeatedly.

Our course would follow northwest as we wended our way through Kattegat and thence around the Skaw. With the winds fair, they would remain so while my wife was with them, I expected that we should round the Skaw in a couple of days. Until then, there was little to do. Happily, the old Jarl was up to the task of keeping me entertained. His stories about the romantic activities of my grandfather amused me greatly. The crew, not sure what to think of a man of reputed magic whose power was highly regarded by the King, were respectful if cautious and curious;

they listened intently to the Jarl's stories. I can only guess what they thought of me; they probably thought I was a dangerous skin-changer who trafficked in the dark and fell powers; I'm sure rumors abounded; I heard one of the crew say the word *aptraganga,* which refers to an unquiet spirit. I wondered what the men would say if they knew we would be taking a close look at this legend in short order. Indeed, the subject came up after supper when we congregated for a group palaver. Usually, a crew would not be so familiar with their jarl, but Jarl Hakon was their leader for so long that very few men could recall a time when he was NOT the man in charge; I was asked some very pointed questions.

Jarl Hakon Harefoot

"Tell me, Master Arn, we have heard our Jarl speak of your grandfather, who must have been a mighty warrior and wizard, defeating the man they call the *King of Death*. Of course, I have heard stories about such creatures, but not how they come to exist."

"The undead, referred to as after-walkers, are usually men who have died under certain conditions. First of all, they die with their eyes open, which is not a common thing, although it happens. Then too, they must die sitting up and be part of a quarrel between father and son, which is common enough. These are the peculiar conditions associated with these creatures though I have often wondered what these things have to do with becoming a restless spirit."

"It is said that they ride animals. Is that true?" asked another man.

"I have heard that too," I replied, "they also have blue faces. I've even heard the claim that two of them worked together to kill animals and people. They often live in the mounds where they were buried and come out at night to raid the countryside. That is where I earn my bread because my runes and spells keep the dead in the ground; my spells prevent dark powers from being used to raise them besides the usual grave robbers." Here I paused for wine to be brought. There was no good way of avoiding such talk, especially on a peculiar voyage like ours. Perhaps it was best to put the truth out in the open and let men understand the dark forces we must contend with.

"As far as the *King of the Dead* is concerned," I said, resuming the topic of the restless corpses, "he did not create true aptraganga. He controlled the dead at all hours of the day and night, in numbers great and small. He used complicated and hard-to-find spells with his inborn ability. Had he hired more warriors to his numbers, he would have been more successful; as it was, he didn't consider that another man of magic could swing an axe."

"Ha! If only you could have been there," interjected the Jarl, "He was a sight to see! Do you know what they called him? No? He was known as *Gudgaest Ox-Back or Gudgaest Hammer-Fist*."

"We shouldn't lose sight of the fact that the so-called King of the Dead killed hundreds of people. First, he drugged them with a poppy-laced wine, and then he poisoned them by convincing them to eat the rotted flesh of his earlier victims. They died horrible deaths full of pain and misery. Then he recalled them to a shadow life where they became ravers every bit as insane as he was." I said, hoping to instill a sense of earnestness in our discourse.

"So, your grandfather was called the Hammer Fist?" asked a man as he looked at my lean arms.

"Have you ever killed a wizard before?" Another one asked. "It is said that we are going to Scandia so that you can kill such a man who uses dark forces against the king."

"How many battles have you fought in?" wondered another voice. I was being pelted by difficult questions faster than I could answer them. The Jarl saw what was happening; in a commanding voice, he called the crew's attention to the fact that the winds shifted, making the sail need trimming as it flapped idly. He told them to keep a better eye on the wind, or he would put them to the oars. After this, I decided that I would have to be more careful about what I said in future conversations. When I told Jarl Hakon about this later, he said he had a better idea. Leave the crew out altogether when talking about magic. He maintained that while there were many intelligent individuals on board, collectively, they had the mentality of a herd of goats.

"The time will come when we'll have to have some straight talk with the crew. But let's not worry them any sooner than we have to. Remember, these men have made a living using their hands, not their minds."

Soon we reached the Skaw; with our backs to the wind in clear skies, we made good time. The following morning, we heard horns blow from the ships in front of us. Jarl Hakon ordered our horns blown in reply; he told the helmsman to continue sailing west and north, following the land on our right, the two following ships keeping pace. The King's ships headed southwest, keeping the land of the Jutes on their left. At this division of the forces, the crew expressed surprise, but as the Jarl saw fit to make no announcement, they kept to their duties with their mouths shut.

I had sailed enough to know that the pleasures on board a ship are few. Sleeping on a heaving, uneven deck is difficult. So is pissing over the rail. Washing one's ass in salt water is no fun either, and for the first couple of days, the smell of vomit was always present; I wasn't seasick, but others were. That included some that I would have thought were immune to such things.

As the days passed, we saw very few other ships. Those we did come across didn't linger when they saw three ships loaded with men. When we were five days out of Roskilde, the old Jarl ordered all ships to land in Scandia at the village of Viksalla; here, we would take on fresh water and buy supplies if we could.

The Jarl expressed surprise at not seeing anyone as we sailed for shore. The fields were empty, with nobody to be seen around and the fishing boats pulled up on shore; nor was there a dog to be seen or grazing goats. Crew members gave each other sidelong looks as they wondered what this meant.

While the men took on water from a quick-moving stream, the Jarl and I, along with a strong detachment of warriors, made our way to the village that lay within wooden walls a hundred paces or so from the ships. Here we found the gate closed, which we expected, of course. We called out, saying we didn't want to rob them or even enter their village; we just wanted information and to buy produce if we could; we had silver to pay with. But all was saw was the furtive face of a youth on the wall who began to weep and wail at the mere sight of us before running off. All we could do was look at each other and shrug our shoulders. We didn't dare enter the village, although there was nothing to prevent us from knocking down the gate. The danger of plague, a possible explanation for this odd circumstance, made us keep our distance. It was possible that everyone on the other side of that gate was either sick or dying. Or maybe there was another reason. There was just no way to know without using my magical abilities, which I was loath to do; I didn't want to advertise my coming with a show of magic. There could be eyes upon us at this very moment; let's not reward them with anything like useful information. After we returned to the ships, the Jarl ordered food to be served for only the Gods; he proclaimed, knew when we could eat on dry land again. As we ate, he spoke to us.

"My comrades and friends, both old and new, I have brought you a long way from home. We have reached a point where you deserve an explanation of why we are here and what we hope to accomplish. I have a few things to say, after which I will call upon my friend and servant to the King, Master Arn Jensson, to give his opinion on what we can expect in the days ahead. Now, let's pass the wineskins around, and I'll tell you what's on my mind." Here the old Jarl took a long pull on the wine sack before passing it to the next man.

"You have all heard the rumors about the ship we sent to Scandia a year ago to investigate claims that a new evil had sprung up. This is true. The exact place is unknown, but we believe it to be at the end of a very long fjord. For quite some time, no word was heard as to their fate. Then traders, men who can be trusted, found their ship at the entrance to that same fjord." Here he stopped and looked down in deep thought for a short time before continuing. "The men were dead, no doubt you know that. You may not be familiar with other dreadful facts, however. They had been killed somewhere else, brought back to the ship in a mutilated condition, then hands were nailed to the oars, feet to the decks, and their balls shoved in their mouths. About the ship, various incantations were written in the language of runes, the type known to Master Arn. These were good men," he said, pausing with evident emotion. "I knew some of them. They were not the kind of warriors easily beaten in battle; I simply don't know what could have happened. I hope that soon we will learn who is responsible for this so that we can give every one of them the kind of death they deserve. The King has given us a powerful weapon against possible enchanters and their worthless oath-breaking killers and berserkers who work for them. You are sworn men of honor who respect the Gods and obey our King. In the coming days, we will be tested; you can rely on that. I do not doubt your ability; all I ask is that when the time comes, you obey Master Arn when it comes to matters of magic, just like you obey me when it comes to fighting and sailing. As to the King and his ships, I will let the high servant of the King tell you about that. We face more than one threat; it is through Arn's skill that we know of this."

At this, I stood up and nodded to the Jarl, making such laudatory remarks that I thought were appropriate. It took me aback to be called by the patronymic system of names used by many in this part of the world; seldom have I been called *Jensson*.

"My friends and shipmates: It's been my honor to sail among you and share your food and drink. First of all, let me give credit to where credit is due. It was Master Steinson who found the link in the chain of conspiracy that brings us here today. Alas, he was killed for his trouble. He will be avenged; do not doubt that for an instant. The two men who died in torment at the harbor were only the first payment. It's true they killed my friend, yet they only acted on orders from others. Be that as it may, a group of pirates and cutthroats have banded together to strike Roskilde while the King and his ships went north. That is why we divided the fleet in the way we did. As the King sails south along the coast of the Jutes, the ships of the pirate scum sail north. If the Gods favor us, the creatures of the deep will feast on many corpses in the days to come if they haven't already. I would give ten marks of gold to see the look on their faces when they find the King and his men bearing down on them." This got quite a laugh.

"As to our situation here, we have less information. We know that a type of forbidden magic has been used here. But we don't know for sure who is using it. I have seen the web, but not the spider. Perhaps it is the assistant to the former King of the Dead, maybe not. I avoid guessing about what may or may not be without facts. I can tell you," I said, turning so that my gaze fell upon everyone in turn, "that those who use this kind of magic are insane. They may look like humans, but their souls are those of ravening beasts. They do not control the magic; the magic controls THEM. Beyond this, let me tell you that they rely on fear to sap your strength and eat away at your loyalty. They will create fearsome illusions in your mind; you'll see things that will freeze your blood. Some of this I can fight against with my own gifts. Also, I bring a potion I will give you to drink when I think the time is right; it will clear your mind and strengthen you. Be warned, though; it has a sour taste. One last thing," I said with hands folded in front of me, "we must remain vigilant. The biggest danger to us is being ambushed; that might have happened to the ship sent here last year. Keep a close watch, especially at night."

The following day, late in the afternoon, we sailed through the islands scattered about the entrance to the fjord we were looking for. The Jarl told of farms and a small village we would pass nearby. Indeed, we did sail near these fields and buildings; not a soul was seen or a wisp of smoke coming from any building. The fjord entrance itself was broad, with mountains on either side. It was also empty, not a ship to be seen. I noted that the weather was cooling even before sunset; this made it ripe for fog. I looked at the cages of the falcons we brought and wondered.

"Jarl Hakon," I said, "What say we wait until morning to examine the fjord? The day is almost spent."

"Spent and getting colder by the moment, we'll have fog soon; this is no time to try your wings, Master Arn. We'll stand out to sea tonight; in the morning, we will see what we can see. The way looks wide and straight from here, but once in the fjord, you'll see how it twists and bends like a snake." The delay until morning was fine with me; I wanted to see where we were going. It was a shame we couldn't go on shore, but it was too dangerous. Still, I missed having a fire, but I reflected for the hundredth time that comfort is not found at sea.

The morning brought a dampness that made the old sailors curse for bringing back bad humors to their bones. It didn't last, though, as the sun's rays soon burned off the fog. After eating my morning bread, I talked to the King's bird man. The Falcons had to be fed enough so they wouldn't take off and go hunting on their own, but not so much that they felt inclined to fly to the nearest branch for a nap. I had done this business once before, and while I liked it for what I could see, I found that a pinfeather itch can be uncomfortable.

There was no hiding this from the crew, they stood watching as the Jarl, the bird fellow, and I stood in the bow. The sail was lowered with the men at the oars to keep us from drifting too far. I selected the smaller of the two males as he seemed less agitated. The Jarl handed me my stone bottle. I unstopped the top taking a long swig of the Black Drink. No doubt I made a face, for I could see the old Jarl smile. I sat on the deck with my back against the rowing bench, waited, and gave a short nod. The handler released the bird that circled the ship in a low spiral, then suddenly headed for the entrance to the fjord. This ability was one of the more important things I learned from my adventure atop the north tower roof. Whatever the discomfort from itching feathers, the view made up for it.

I rapidly gained altitude with the help of the brisk mountain breezes. When I got high enough, I soared with little help from my wings. I saw few other birds; most were just gulls, far below me. The bird minder had cautioned me about eagles; they were the only things that could bother me at this height. If indeed I was pestered by an eagle, he thought I should be able to outfly it.

For over an hour, I flew straight east down the middle of the fjord, which snaked its way forward as far as I could see. I wasn't sure how far I went, but it was about as much we could sail in a day if we had the wind. At the moment, the land breeze was against us though; perhaps at night, we could use the sail, but the Jarl warned me that winds inside the bigger fjords were fickle and couldn't be depended on, for now, we had to rely on the speed of our oars and the strength of our crew. Thankfully I was exempt from a turn at the oars; my energy would be needed for other things, such as flapping these wings. Turning back, I began a long slow decline with a quick circle every so often to look behind. Eventually, I landed on the arm of the keeper, my mind once more back in my body. The fact that I came safely back brought out smiles from the crew. Later in the afternoon, I would make another quick flight, for I wanted no surprises.

"Have you seen any dragons?" asked the Jarl as we sat and talked after my return.

"Nay, not a single one; I saw the seal-hunting whales, big grey whales, and many dolphins, but no dragons. Nor do I wish to see one; even beholding a dragon from a distance is too close for me. But how can any dragons be left if you count the number our heroes killed in our songs and sagas? I wonder that the minstrels don't claim one for you, my Jarl."

"They would do so if I paid them more. Unlike some of these puffed-up warriors of the feasting table and the long drinking bench, I don't need to hear flattery. Especially if I must pay for it. But tell me, my young hunting bird, don't you get dizzy from flying so high?"

"No, it feels very natural. I thought it would be difficult, but once I knew I could see from the bird's eyes, the rest was easy. I enjoyed it."

"Did you sense any magic? There are no people here, not a single one, no sign of anything. We should have seen a man, cow, or ship by now."

"I felt no magic, but you are very right, my Jarl," I said as I turned to study the north edge of the fjord, "there is naught here. Before dark, I will have another look; that way, we can sleep more easily, should we sleep at all." Later that afternoon, I made another trip upwards into the beautiful sky that overlooked this part of Scandia. There were no farms on the sides of the fjord at this point. The land consisted of heavily forested mountainsides or the rubble of rocks that had fallen from greater heights. There was no life to be seen, not even mountain goats. Only within the fjord were signs of life as great schools of herring went by us as bigger predators chased them. At dusk, the breeze changed direction; it blew straight down the fjord. With the sail stretched to its fullest, we rode at our best speed by the rising moon's light. There was little sleep for me, though; I ordered that I should be woken at the start and the middle of each watch. It was time to be wary and look about, even if only to piss and sniff the night air. As for the hairy star, which we had seen for so long, we ceased talking about it, continued to move across the sky at night, its tail slowly changing direction. Mad men and mad women gave many opinions as to what was going on. Prudent people ignored such rumors, yet my father once told me that the old priests of the Gauls believed that these stars would return over the years at intervals. He said they could forecast their appearance, which often coincided with bad harvests and sickness. Tonight, with the sky exceptionally clear, the star appeared to be turning from pink to blue mixed with white. As beautiful as the night sky was, I roused myself, remembering that there was work to be done before I could rest. Most importantly, I needed to mix a big batch of the Black Drink. I was counting on this elixir to stiffen the crew's spirits if we had to face magic. After fetching my satchel of supplies, I sat on an oar bench talking to a couple of crewmen who came from a north island of the Danes. They were happy to hear that this brew would protect them from the curses of magicians. It was also proof against the bites of wolves, trolls, ghosts, and unclean spirits. This, of course, they were also glad to hear; I hoped it would not be put to the test as I had doubts about the utility of the drink used in such circumstances. Only to raise the confidence of the crew was I willing to endorse such claims.

The rest of the night was unremarkable; The Black Drink was mixed, strained, and stored in a small barrel. Later I would split it up into separate flasks for the three ships. Then I could get some sleep in fits and starts until daylight when I ate bread with the Jarl. We talked about the prospects for the day, which were a mystery to both of us. The wind had died, so the Jarl put the men to the oars for a while. He would keep them there just long enough to get the aches and pains driven out of the joints. The Danes were firm believers in exercising to get rid of joint pain. I doubted that very much, as the only thing that exercise gave me was more pain. They were also big believers in drinking wine at the start of the day; that was an idea more to my liking.

The following day was merely a repetition of the first; winds out of the east by day, the opposite at night. The only difference was the temperature; it was getting colder by the hour. By the morning of the third day, it looked like a thunderstorm could strike sooner rather than later. I began to suspect that something else might strike us as well; I noticed the odd tingling at the back of my neck, the same as I felt the day we were attacked at the farmhouse. Are we being watched? The men with the sharpest eyesight were put in the bow of each ship. Jarl Hakon sat sharpening his axe while talking to the blade as if it were a living being. I had heard of this strange habit that the warriors among the Danes practiced in this regard. They tried to reach their weapon's spirit, which I regarded odd. I doubted it was possible to commune with a piece of sharpened iron any more than one could hold debates with an oil lamp. I said nothing, regardless of my thoughts on the matter. The world is full of odd and childish thinking; I heard my father talk of something similar once. Germans would speak to their spears before battle as if they were living beings. While the Jarl was thus occupied, I took a quick look ahead from the sky. It was better to do this now due to the possibility of rain.

The visibility was good enough for the moment, for I could see far ahead. It wouldn't last, though; from my height, which was about the same as those of the smaller mountains, I could see a squall line heading our way. What was hidden behind it, I couldn't tell. Something was approaching, though; I could feel it in my mind; I attempted to probe the hidden force with magic but failed. I flew lower back and forth across the gradually narrowing fjord. There had to be magic involved, that much I knew; beyond this, I was baffled. Staying aloft would serve no purpose, so I returned to the ship. As I landed on the outstretched arm of the falcon handler, I noticed that the Jarl had ordered his ships to sail all three abreast rather than in line. Perhaps that made better sense in a storm. I'd have to rely on his judgment regarding things like that. The sails were lowered due to the swirling wind's uncertain direction and the approaching rain. Just as the oars were being run out, I thought I could hear the first distant peal of thunder. Suddenly I remembered the Black Drink; I had almost forgotten it! Taking the small flask from my belt, I took a quick gulp; I yelled to the Jarl's servant to get the flask I gave him to keep for the crew. Then I stood on the prow with my leg braced by the dragon's head; with a quick motion, I signaled to the other ships to drink the brew as instructed. Each man was to get a quick gulp, no more, no less. In this matter, I was making history of a sort. Never had the Black Drink been shared with others; this jealously guarded secret was never intended for the uninitiated; my grandfather would have fainted to see such a thing. Yet I could think of nothing else to do in a circumstance we will likely face. Certainly, it was a risk, how much so we would soon find out. I could see no ill effect for the moment as I looked around at the faces straining forward in anticipation of some action. I saw the Jarl standing near the bow leaning to the side to view the approaching storm. Like everyone else, he suspected some danger was lurking behind the approaching gloom. Again, I heard a crack of lightning; my eyes looked dead ahead like everyone else's. Somehow that didn't seem right; I was missing something, then I turned my head towards the ship's stern. The noise that I made was later compared to how a boar might sound after seeing the farmer's wife approaching with a castrating knife in her hand. While we concentrated on the danger ahead, a monstrous Kraken with tentacles twice as long as the ship approached us from behind.

Others, too, cried out when they looked behind us. The exception was the man at the tiller who suddenly clutched at his throat, turned blue, fell forward and died on the spot quicker than it takes to tell about it. That caused the ship to lurch dangerously close to another ship. Jarl Hakon was on it with bounds that would have been amazing for a man half his age. With a grab and a shove, he took control of the tiller and barked orders. Half the crew bent the oars as the rest notched arrows or took spears; for myself, I made my way to the rear post of the ship. I could hear the monster roaring with the sound of hundreds of bellowing oxen. Bracing myself as best I could, I started tracing the runes in my mind and then doing the same with my finger in the air in front of me. The power transferred from my mind to my hands came much slower than I wished. It took a great effort not to fall victim to the fear that was trying to seize control of me; for an instant, I wanted to jump overboard. I could feel the eyes of the creature, the whites of which were as large as a shield, boring into me. By the time I had finished the first rune, the beast was scarce a boat length behind us. It appeared it would come between us and the middle ship, the size of its tentacles sufficient to drive us to the bottom of the fjord with a single blow.

Now came the test as the magic of the red-hot runes in the air crackled like the sound of pork skins fried in an iron pan. With a flick of my wrist, I tossed a rune of power between the eyes of the hideous creature. Without waiting for the result, I put my mind to work creating another. My effort immediately stopped as I heard a noise so loud as to almost flatten me on the deck. The rune that flew from my hand would have landed between the eyes of the creature just as I had thrown it. But the

Kraken had no eyes; it was all an illusion with no more substance than my chalk drawings of the new palace. The whole thing began to burn as soon as the rune hit it; in the blink of an eye, it glowed with tattered remnants either blown away by the wind or falling into the water.

The crew looked around dumbly; nobody had any idea of what had just happened. One moment we were in danger of being killed by the most feared of all sea monsters; the next moment, it was gone. It was obvious that a form of magic had been used against us. Not the sort of magic tricks meant to entertain those at feasts either. No, this magic was there to kill us.

As for the storm that approached, it died at the same time the Kraken did. There was naught to it but a few drops of rain and gusts of wind; it, too, was an illusion. The Jarl declared that we needed to land and regroup; he spied a patch of sandy beach on the north side that could serve our purpose. With oars bent to a slow and somewhat shaky cadence, we made our way to the bank of the fjord. I was only too eager at that point to jump over the side when the keel of our ship scraped bottom. Taking a rope in hand, I helped pull the ship forward. The Jarl told me later that in all of his adventures, he had never seen men so glad to stand on solid ground. As I expected, the men turned to me for guidance, so I spoke to them about what had just transpired and a bit about rune magic. The Jarl, though, plied a shovel for his friend who had died at the tiller when the attack began. The Jarl was strange in this respect; another man would have made somebody else dig. He was also reputed to execute criminals personally as they did in the old days; his leadership was direct, a trait that he shared with King Bjornson.

"We saw a strange sight today; if I knew what it was, I'd be telling you a lie. We were attacked; there is no doubt of it. Whoever is against us will try again, that we may be sure of. As we saw a short time ago, anyone with the power to raise such a specter won't be easily defeated. But I think," I said as I looked them over, "That the potion I gave you helped you resist the urge to panic; it was no joke; I felt that urge to flee myself. The spell was powerful, but so were the runes; I needed to look ahead before we went any further. But that will have to wait until the morrow, for we can do no more today. Until daybreak, we need to eat and rest, except for those unlucky enough to stand watch." At this, I walked away from the men to where the Jarl was digging, in the failing light, a grave for his friend.

"You make a good speaker, better than me; alas, my voice is no longer suited to talk in front of many." He said this as he began to shovel sand on the body. I reached over and took the shovel from his hand; he was too spent for work like this.

"I thought you Danes always left grave goods," I said, "not to be critical, of course."

"I will give his money and armor to his sons; they will do more good with it than putting them in the ground. Besides, I am not so sure that Odin will take him. He might, for this man could fight very well; he proved that many times, but he didn't die in battle. He fell over from a fright that might not be considered a good way to go.

One can never tell from the stories told of the Gods. But I must leave you now and sleep, or I, too, will be joining the Gods. I don't understand what happened today, only that I am exhausted; thank you for lending a hand." I finished burying the man, piling a small mound of stones over his grave before bidding him a last farewell. Then I went to sleep onboard the ship, the land too damp for me.

We were up early to cook a meal on solid ground, which is much easier than doing it on the deck of a ship, although you can get sand on your plate if you're not careful. We wasted no time getting the food down our gullets; now that the magic wielder had shown his hand, there was no reason for him to wait. No, we would be attacked again as soon as it suited his malevolent purpose. That purpose must be discovered; once again, I prepared myself to look through the eyes of a bird.

My wings beat quickly as I pushed myself to gain altitude as the men pushed the ships back into the water. The fjord went forward for a short distance before taking a sharp jog to the north, followed by an abrupt turn in the opposite direction. The Jarl told me that this was called *the notch* by the locals. In the distance, I could see where the fjord finally split in two, leaving a triangle of land between them. The Jarl told me that this was the beginning of farmland as the mountains quickly decreased in height. Also visible were the deltas of rivers that wended their way into the fjord. It was a scene of outstanding natural beauty, yet something in the distance was wrong; I could tell from this distance that the lands were covered in heavy fog, but it was a fog that was moving westward *against* the wind. As it progressed, it grew denser; the areas surrounding the river deltas, clearly visible just a short time ago, were now lost in a thick misty haze.

After seeing what was to be seen, I returned to the ship to tell them what I'd observed. Then prepare as best we could for whatever was coming. I could only hope that any monsters dredged up from the deep would be similar to what we faced the previous day and not the more substantial kind.

I found the ships lined up just past the entrance to the notch; their sails had been furled as the winds inside this place are notorious, the Jarl said, for being changeable. On either side stood lofty cliffs of sheer rock, wide in some areas, narrow in others. After I made my report about the approaching fog, the Jarl ordered the rowing speed increased; he wanted to avoid being trapped in this narrow strait.

The Jarl alternated giving men short breaks to catch their breath, piss, and drink water. While I was helping to hand out dippers of water, the Jarl asked me what I thought we could expect.

"That would be most difficult to guess because we are dealing with unusual abilities. What we saw with the fake Kraken would have been enough to break the minds of many crews. Thank the God of Thunder that your men are experienced and not easily frightened. The drink helped, too, I think. I will tell you plainly that I still have no idea who is behind this; we may wish my grandfather was here with us before this day is done."

"The coming fog worries me," he said quietly, "it must be made by a wizard; there is no other way to account for it. We must find this man and split his skull open."

"I couldn't agree more," I said, gripping his shoulder as I walked back, "I don't think I have my grandfather's strength when it comes to using an axe, but by the nine worlds, I'd give it a try."

The rock walls of the straights towered above us as we sailed dead north to where we would soon make the turn that would have us reverse direction for a mile or more. Once through this pinched and twisted passage, we could resume our course back to due east, although we are beginning to run out of fjord. According to the Jarl, this region was notorious for ships getting smashed against the rocks from swirling winds, tides, storms, and, perhaps, wizardry.

As we rounded the top of the slot, a sudden stillness occurred. The wind died; the sea calmed; the silence hung so heavy I felt half afraid to speak. Then we saw it; a thick green and yellowish mist; it spread forward like some disease completely engulfing ships. It happened so quickly that there was nothing that we could do to evade it. Our ship was the first to be covered in this unwholesome fog, but the others were quickly swallowed up, much to the horror of their crews. The Jarl ordered the men to pay attention to their oars and for the ships to close up the space between each other and to have our weapons at hand. He also bid the man at the tiller to count the oar strokes and make a hard turn left when we got to 200 strokes. He reckoned that we would be far enough south in the notch to turn east by then. Beyond that, he whispered to me that he had run out of ideas. His concern was wasted on me, though, for I had no ideas either. This is how the situation remained until we had gone far enough for an abrupt turn east. But just as the ships had made the turn, something happened that made the sailors drop their oars while they looked forward in consternation.

Abruptly a huge torso began to come together directly in front of us. It was made from the wisps and tendrils of the fell-looking fog. It reminded me of an idol dedicated to the God of War I once saw on a household altar in Rus with its war helmet, long braided hair, bushy eyebrows, and beard that reached its waist. In one hand, it clenched a short, broad-bladed spear; in the other, a thick whip.

With its eyes grotesquely bulged open, this apparition towered in front of us, every bit as fearsome as the Kraken we had encountered before. Then I could see its lips begin to quiver, followed by the jaw that started moving about as if it was trying to talk. As this happened, frothy black blood started leaking between its lips. Then came a tearing sound as its mouth ripped open to show a row of short stumpy blood-soaked teeth, followed by a loud voice that spat forth blood and words.

"Why has King Bjornson sent you? We have no need for goat fucking men in these parts. Take your crew of wart-covered, walrus-faced dung-eaters home. The crazy man who chisels dirty pictures on stones with his tools is not wanted either; his magic is worthless, just like the whore he's married to. Get you gone or feel the fire of my death magic; the Kraken was only a toy to amuse me; come further, and you will see real monsters. There are no dragon killers among you, are there? Or troll killers? Can anyone among your scum kill those who are already dead? Tell your King that this land is not his or for the cowards that serve him. All who go further will die by fire and ice, but only after we have ripped out their tongues and eaten their eyes."

After these words were said, the creature of mist began to dissolve. For a while, everyone stood in silence, looking at each other. Nobody had any idea what to say. Nor did anyone, me included, know how seriously such an insult should be taken.

The Jarl was not a man to sit idly by in the face of a threatened attack. He called his men back to the oars. He intended to put us on land at the point where the fjord divides; from there, we could send out scouting parties, and I could search the sky. The mist creature mentioned a dragon; I wanted to see if that was true. Much depended on how long this fog could be kept up; it must be a function of magic, so it had a limit to how long it could last. But how long it would take for that limit to be reached was unknown; still, going ashore was the right move; I'd rather face magic with my feet on solid ground. As we plowed ahead to a steady beat, I suddenly felt very relaxed; sitting on the deck with my back against the side of the ship, my mind began to drift.

"Look who's come to eat at my table," said the man to nobody in particular. "It's the young pup wanting to suckle at the teat of wisdom. Mayhap this old cow has run dry of that particular kind of milk." the old man said as he laughed. "I know too what they say about those who laugh too long and loudly at their own jokes. But this is my dream as much as it's yours, thank you! When you get to my age, one can laugh as much as he wants."

"Good to see you, grandfather," I said as I exhaled deeply. "We could use your help; a wizard is seeking to slay us. He says he has a dragon."

"Does he now? If that's true, you're in a terrible spot. But so is he; can you imagine how much it must cost him a month to feed it?"

"Maybe he sends his dragon out to fend for itself; there are always fish in the fjord," I said as I looked around at the idols rich in gems and gold and the shaven-headed priests dressed in white; it was plain to see that we were standing in the great temple at Uppsala. I have never been there, but from travelers' descriptions, this could be no other place. As I looked around, my grandfather took from an elaborately carved wooden dish a pinch of fragrant resin; placing his hand to his nose, he breathed deeply before casting the substance into the hearth, where it vanished in a puff of fragrant smoke.

"If I wanted to know if the Gods exist, would I first go to the priests for an answer?" he asked teasingly.

"I'm sure that many people would start by doing just that," I said, pausing to think well aware of the traps my grandfather liked to lay in our sessions, "but they couldn't be objective about such a question. Could they? If they renounced the Gods, how would they get their bread? You told me in our last meeting to look at the nature of things."

"And so, I did, my young pup," he said with a smile as he walked over to view a representation of the Goddess Frigg, mother of Thor, "I'm happy to hear that you have had the good sense to think about my ramblings. But nothing I have said is not to be found between your own two ears. You know these things either from your own experiences, what your father had told you, and the few things that I could tell you before I came here, the other side of life and existence. But let us not debate," he continued as he bowed to Frigg and kept walking down the great hall of idols, "the nature of the Gods, such questions that are best talked about while fishing." At this, he laughed a time much longer than needed.

"Why have we come to the home of the Gods then, my grandfather?"

"Home? There is no home for the Gods in mid-earth. They are now feasting in Asgard with the victorious dead."

"Why are they called the victorious dead?" I asked. These souls are often the defeated ones in battle. The ones better at fighting returned home to feast and father children."

"Perhaps you are right, but the sagas don't see it that way. But those who die in battle and are not selected have a much more difficult time;

they are very unfortunate. Nobody cares about their fate; they are never mentioned or thought of." As he said this, he put a finger aside his nose and looked me in the eye significantly.

"You mean the Dragenin? Those who perished in battle but were not found worthy to enter the feasting halls of the dead?" At this, I couldn't repress a shudder at the thought of these unquiet souls usually mentioned in hushed voices by those who tell fearful winter tales.

"Yes, that is who I mean. These spirits are in no hurry to become part of the afterlife, where they exist in a shade-like existence. Until they are gathered and taken below, they wander aimlessly, feeling nothing but a dull, numbing cold. They hate the living whom they avoid. There are thousands of them wandering the woods of these parts, also in swamps and burial grounds, but they can't be seen by ordinary eyes, of course, so not much attention is given to them."

"Does anyone have the ability to command such creatures?" I wondered half to myself as he stopped before a carved representation of Braggi, the God of poetry and rune masters like me; he was born with runes of song on his tongue.

"Beyond the Valkyrie and the Gods, only the Swart dwarfs can command these creatures. The Swart dwarfs are not sociable creatures; they despise humans, and all of their thinking involves scheming and plotting to gain an advantage over us." "Their greed is legendary, but what have they to do with us?" I asked, turning to look him in the eye. "Any time that you find an evil and complicated plot look for the Swart dwarfs; while few of their schemes have ever worked, they are still dangerous," said the old man as he nodded to a passing priest whose inked eyes made him look like a thin bear coming out after hibernation. "But what in the nine worlds would bring them here at the end of this fjord? For gold? Nobody has ever found any in these parts; there are no riches here, only some farms."

"Indeed, there is little here to tempt either raiders or wizards, yet here we are. Let's sit; my legs are tired; the priests will give us wine; they owe me favors, as do the Gods." Here he laughed heartily for what must have been some secret joke. Nonetheless, after we sat on a bench against the wall, the priests brought us wine in silver cups.

"If we put aside the stumbling and bumbling dead or almost dead, you have become suspicious of the so-called facts you've found. You've been thinking about the obvious difference in the stories you've told by those who have fled from these parts and the reality of what you have seen. Things don't quite add up, do they?"

"No, grandfather, they don't. Those stories cannot be any more real than the Kraken that appeared to us. Yet those who beheld the terrors sweeping down upon them didn't doubt that what they saw was real. They believed, beyond any doubt, that great numbers of the undead were swarming out of this fjord, over-running farms with great slaughter. They saw numbers of hairy-faced men riding wolves. Yet the population here is small; there are not enough dead, even if added to the living, to bring such numbers. Nor are there large populations anywhere else close at hand. Even among the Danes, such an avalanche of dead warriors would be difficult to explain. From the start, this has been a question in my mind. This Kraken exposed some deceptions, yet to make a widespread delusion would be an even greater feat of magic."

"So, you are reduced to the age-old question of how to separate truth from falsehood, reality from imagination, perhaps even sanity from madness. You are in quite a predicament, that's for sure. And now you must leave me. You must wake up; a dragon is coming. If you kill it, I suppose I will have to write a saga about you. Will my labors never end? I suggest that you tie the ships together in the middle. The dragon will seek to separate and kill you, one ship at a time."

As he said this to me, my shoulder was shaken, and I was yanked to my feet. The old Jarl was pointing and gesticulating; following his pointed finger, I saw a light in the distance just off the left bow.

"That's a dragon, a dragon is coming, by the hammer!" he shouted in my ear.

"Put the ships together, lashed amidships," I shouted, "Don't argue; Gudgaest says to do it." The mention of my grandfather made the old man's eyes open wide with wonder, but there was no time for explanations. He ordered the ships to be brought together and tied with cables.

No shape could yet be determined as the light went this way and that way in search of us. Apparently, not even dragons had great vision in thick fog. Soon we would lose the daylight, but I couldn't be sure if this helped or hindered us. Men grabbed armor and arms in preparation for what was to come. Yet I had very little knowledge of what I would do. Without thinking, I grabbed the last of the Black Drink from my belt. With a quick motion, I took out my small knife and cut the end of my finger deep enough to make the blood shoot out; then, I began to recite a childhood charm my father taught me; in fact, it was the first I had ever learned. It was a protection charm. My father was a firm believer in them; this one was good for keeping spirits from hiding under my bed, I recalled. As I mumbled the charm, I began to assemble the runes in my mind.

We could see the beast's shape through the mist when it found us. Shoving its head forward half a boat length, it glared down on the ships. It had a spiral-shaped horn on the tip of its snout just above a line of teeth, each longer than my arm. In the middle of what could have been its forehead was a single malevolent lidless eye from which a beacon of piercing white light shone. Suddenly the dragon's head whipped around as it wheeled upwards. Obviously, it was going to gain some altitude from which to open its attack on us. As it turned away, working its wings faster and faster, I began to prepare, as did the crew. I saw men holding their bows, ready to draw them as the creature neared.

"Aim for his eye," bellowed the Jarl as we watched the beast wheel and turn toward us, which I reckoned was a good deal longer than the ship. As brave as these men were, I suspect that most would have rather heard him shout *over the rail and swim for shore!*

I was more of a spectator than a participant, for my mind was reeling as the magic formed within me. My mouth seldom stopped as I recited verses of poetic charms as the runes shifted and drifted across the range of my mental vision. Runes formed into groups and colors; some looked like they had been carved on the faces of gigantic cliffs, while others acted like little birds that flitted in and out of my hands. They hung in front of me, pulsating with invisible heat and power. No doubt, the crew thought that I'd gone mad; the runes would not have been visible to them, and it would have looked like I was poking and drawing in the empty air while uttering incomprehensible sounds.

When the dragon had reached a sufficient height, it made a sharp wheel almost directly overhead—seeing this, our leader called for everyone but the archers under their shields. A question formed in my mind, did all dragons shoot fire? The reply, at least as far as this dragon was concerned, was not long in coming. I could see its upper throat begin to glow. Immediately my arms shot upward as I summoned a small but intense rune that I shot at the beast, it missed, but the accompanying blast of air laid the dragon on its side; while it was off balance, I struck again and again, like invisible fists punching its side. This did no significant damage in itself, but it ended any attacks on us from directly above. Dripping with sweat, I took some deep breaths as the beast retreated. As we watched, a crew member cried out, "next, our wizard will shoot lightning bolts from out of his ass!" As scared as everyone was, all had a good laugh at this.

The laughs died out as the dragon resumed his attack, this time from astern. Weaving back and forth, he made for our ships looking like a giant snake as his head rose and fell. During this time, I had not been idle; I took a spear by the shaft and pushed it forward while turning it around in my hands. The runes wrapped themselves around the head, causing it to smoke from the heat. Then when I judged the creature to be within range, I threw it as hard as I could. The magic caused it to sail far beyond my usual range; as it flew over the stern of the ship, I could see the tip of it burst into flame. Then it struck the dragon's head; I heard a thunderous roar; like Thor's hammer, it hit with a crushing blow; the force of the explosion knocked some of the men from off their feet and singed the beards of others. As for the dragon, only a stump remained of the head; the body splashed into the sea, where it sank out of sight quickly, leaving only a few dirty white scales floating on the surface.

As exuberant as I was from this victory, I could no longer keep to my feet. The last thing I remember is men carrying me to an oar bench. In times long after this event, poems would be written about the lengthy battle I had fought with the horned dragon. Mention was made of my great skill with a two-handed sword and my ability to throw a huge axe the length of a ship. But in truth, the battle was short, with no thrusts of a sword given by me or anyone else. We were fortunate, as I told the

Jarl later; for the fates were fickle, very much so when it came to magical contests. One could never be entirely sure in advance which spells will work.

Although our triumph over the one-eyed dragon was complete, the Jarl wisely decided to retreat. There was no danger to navigation, for the fog began to lift as soon as the dragon died. We pulled up on a finger of sand and made campfires out of driftwood. I lay close to the fire, alternately freezing and sweating while the Jarl's men enjoyed a muted celebration. We had no idea what would come, so we kept the watch alert; victory drinks were few, everyone was too tired.

The next morning, feeling revived by a meal of fried salt pork and flatbread washed down by water from a nearby brook, I decided to chance a flight to see if my bird eyes could discover anything more about our situation. I could sense no magic anywhere; it seemed like a very ordinary, partly cloudy day in early summer. As for our previous night's encounter, not a trace was seen.

I flew high above the fjord, headed for the split in the water directly ahead. I got as far as the edge of the land when I noticed a deserted hamlet consisting of a few homes and buildings grouped near a dock. The dock was empty except for the hull of a small sunken boat, but what I saw in a nearby meadow alarmed me. I was shocked enough to want to land. I put that thought aside as this could be a trap, nor did I fly any closer; what I saw was sufficient to chill me. After scanning the skies for birds of prey or larger predators like the kind I saw the evening before, I headed back to the ships as fast as I could fly. I made haste to convince the Jarl to get the oars in the water.

"It's a trap," the old man scoffed, "are you sure what you saw was not just another bit of fakery like the Kraken?"

"I almost hope it's a trap," I said with a laugh, "If it's not a trap, then it's going to be very difficult to understand."

By noon we had come ashore close to the deserted hamlet. From the look of things, I doubted anyone had lived here for some time. We formed in a body, with shields and weapons ready while scouts checked the buildings. They confirmed my thinking, for no recent footprints between the houses were to be seen; nobody had been here for a while.

This puzzled us; a mob of a hundred hidden warriors would have been much easier to understand.

Next, we moved to the meadow, where a grim sight awaited us. There, in the middle of a field, a gallows had been erected. Hanging from it was a heavy, short, frog-faced man who might have seen forty winters. His pale and ugly head was shaved, his beard close cut, and his tongue, which was now purple, hung obscenely from his mouth. His hands were bound so tightly behind him that the cords dug into his wrists. Other marks and cuts told us that his last few hours were unpleasant. Around the rude gallows he hung on were the scattered bones of men and animals. Under his body was a barrel that he was no doubt forced to stand while they put the noose around his neck. The barrel had fallen on its side, showing it was filled with scrolls. This shocking display was done with me in mind, for on his body in bright blue paint were runes that faded as soon as I read them. The message was pointed, literally pointed. Ordering everyone back, I took my sword out and shoved the blade deep into his heart. In my mind's eye, I saw this man in parts of his life. I saw how he first came to this area by boat with bags of silver; he paid for fine lodging and the best food. In the daytime, he studied the bags of scrolls and folded parchments he brought. At night he walked under the sky thinking strange thoughts. At other times he raped women he judged too weak to resist him. That almost got him killed by angry fathers and women who were stronger than they looked. Always he studied the ancient writings that he brought with him. To protect himself, he acquired servants, his source of them was the local graveyard, and soon, people began fleeing the area. Then a group of Swart dwarfs became interested in him, which was highly unusual. As a rule, they hated humans and elves, the Gods, animals, and each other. What they *did* love was precious metals and stones that they used to make wondrous objects with. Indeed, their jewelry was highly sought after; they traded their craft's products for things they needed, like grain, cloth, and leather.

Never before had they found a human with such power. They had in themselves the ability to command the dead; they were the Dragenin, those whom the Valkyries had rejected as unworthy of living in the afterlife with Odin in Valhalla. The Swart dwarfs owed a duty to the Gods to herd these unworthy souls to the lower of the nine worlds; this they did but without enthusiasm. They had, of course, heard of the king of the dead who came to grief with his corpse army some years ago in the seas off the coast of the Cours. Hundar said he was a part of this failed conquest and had learned much from that failed attempt. He said he exceeded his former teacher in the magical arts through study, diligence, and higher intelligence. Moreover, he offered to enrich them with great amounts of treasure. Part of his plan required the use of the Dragenin; the Swart dwarfs were only too happy to oblige as they had no use for these tormented spirits. The former apprentice necromancer had previously found a clan of pirates, now based in the Fang Islands, who were willing to plot with him. Between them, they concocted a plan. Hundar, with his magic and his dead minions, would create enough of a nuisance to tempt the King of the Danes to send his forces north to deal with the threat. This force would be destroyed or at least kept busy by magical means until it was too late. The pirate fleet would simultaneously sail north along the west Jutland coast to Kattegat, then on to the now-empty fortifications at Roskilde. For this service, the pirates would reward Hundar and the dwarfs with untold riches. This architect of evil was shrewd enough to know that others could control magic just as he did. So, he organized his agents to penetrate the capital of the Danes. They identified Steinson as a man who could foil his plans; Hundar ordered him killed and his rustic replacement. It's good for me that his agents didn't discover that my grandfather killed his mentor. He might have tried harder if he knew that. Organizing such a plot could not have been easy. The conspirators had very little in common. They were not related to each other in any way, nor did they share a common language. The dwarfs were notoriously taciturn, rude, and suspicious, while the pirates were completely dishonest, bloodthirsty, and fickle. Hundar, of course, was all of those things besides being mad. Because of the different languages and loyalties involved, the pirates employed a mark, usually put on the shoulder, so their people would know one another.

It may not be accurate to say that the plotters had nothing in common. They all found agreement in their dislike of the Christians and their shave-pated priests. For Hundar, this inverted Christian symbol was a great joke that amused him greatly. Once the plot was agreed upon, Hundar began orchestrating the events that he was sure would bring the Danes, and by extension, the entire North, to their collective knees. For several years the unquiet spirits of the dead attacked the living in Scandia, driving them southwards like so many sheep. In their minds, he planted false visions and memories so that they would spread fear among their neighbors and hoped to provoke retaliation from the King of the Danes. This indeed happened, but the former servant of the king of death was befooled; so were his comrades. To his horror, the King of the Worthless, as the dwarfs termed King Bjornson, had brought north not an army to be slaughtered but a magician of power, a man of runes. Since the death of Steinson, they thought themselves safe from magical power being employed by the Danes, but they failed to reckon with his successor.

With the collapse of his plans and knowing as he did the nature of the Swart dwarfs, who were loyal to nobody, this man Hundar attempted to flee. He was caught, killed, and left on display as a token that the dwarfs were done with him. They wanted no further part in this failed venture. They left his body and cursed writings for me to find as a token of their quick retreat and abandonment of this entire project. This man, who undoubtedly thought he was on the threshold of greatness, fell victim to the same fate as his former mentor. As I cleaned my sword off, I invited everyone to gather wood so that I burn this foul excuse for a man and his vile scrolls.

As we stood there watching this evil man burn, we were shocked to see that the flames became dark green when the scrolls caught fire. As they reached his body, they turned yellow; no doubt, I reflected, this was the magic burning. I had seen bodies burn before, and this color was unnatural. But then again, so was the man now being consumed by fire.

The Necromancer's Apprentice

Chapter Six

The Careful King

King Baldur Bjornson sat looking out over the harbor from the deck of his warship. Here, as the sun sank lower in the sky, he could be alone with his thoughts. The throne room was for business as far as he was concerned, and the throne itself, even with cushions to sit on, was not all that comfortable nor private as servants went to and fro cleaning and doing other such work.

The battle with the pirates was hot work while it lasted. He was very happy he caught them unawares, for when the ships came together, he could tell there were veteran warriors among them. Once they were sighted and the wind confused against them, they had no time to put their armor on, which counted strongly against them. Most of them lacked even a leather jerkin, the minimum requirement for a man who wished to survive a fight.

So many of them had swords, long ones, too--made of the best metal. No group of warriors in the north could match that. As a rule, only the well-off men had one because of their expense. The most common weapon was the axe, followed by the spear. In the hands of an expert, such weapons could be deadly, but none matched a sword when it came to killing. Swords were handier than a spear, and the point could carve out a man's liver with a well-aimed thrust, whereas the axe required a backstroke to be delivered. Each of these pirates had a sword, many of which came into the hands of his men following the battle. Not only were they better armed, but something about their appearance gave him pause. Where were they from? Some he saw with their blond locks and large frame were typical sons of the north, but many of them were not. Something about them was different, but he wasn't sure what.

The style of their ships gave him pause, too; they were not the cheaply built coastal craft that was so common in the north. No, these ships had high sides and a raised prow bigger than ours, the ruler mused as he sat there on an oar bench; they were deeper than ours too. He knew fine workmanship when he saw it; these pirate ships were built regardless of expense, but why? Something was wrong; he could feel it in his bones. Pirates were usually scum that was unfit for anything else; nobody would take them raiding, and clipped ears were the norm for such refuse. Their usual craft was old, worn-out, and often leaky. Nor were they ever known to have a fleet; sometimes, they would band together for a common cause, but this was always two or three ships. Fights between pirates were common, especially when dividing booty after a successful encounter. These men were called pirates, yet he knew they were not. He didn't know whom they belonged to, but they weren't the kind of scum you could find in all ports of the Salt Sea, even here in Roskilde. The king put aside his thoughts for a moment as he drank from a skin of wine from the Franks, which, as everyone knows, is the best.

He cast his mind over what he knew of his neighbors near and far. To the west, the big island of the Saxons was held by King Redwald. But it was out of the question for him to covet his lands because of the distance and the fact that he had enough to do to subjugate his near neighbors, who were a collection of various tribes who would rather fight than eat. No, there was nothing in this mystery that involved the Saxon.

Then there were the Franks, who were wealthy and numerous enough to do him harm if they wished. But first, they would have to stop fighting among themselves, which they did with great energy year after year. He always talked to merchants and sailors who went to trade there, always searching for their best wines in exchange for seal skins and fur. But nothing came to his ears that reflected any desire on their part to raid east.

But trouble out of the east was always a possibility; the Cours [the Baltic States] were a warlike race who raided just as the Danes did. But they seldom went far from home, at least so far. But he had a feeling this could change. In the last two years, they raided merchant ships coming from the Rus, each time going out farther into the Salt Sea. He knew that Bormo had a man there; he'd have to ask if he'd heard from him recently. The Cours bear watching, but he could see no link between them and the pirates that supposedly came from some islands south of where he caught them as they sailed north.

He had pondered this question before; how could raiders live on those miserable islands off the west coast of the Angles? What could they find to eat, sand? North of the Angles were the Jutes; those were the two tribes that existed on the big peninsula that stuck out into the Salt Sea like a horse cock. Many had migrated west to the big island of the Saxon King Redwald in the past hundred years; some were still going there. But Bormo had men in the household of every important jarl; if any plans were made, he would know it before their first sail ever left the harbor.

As far as his jarls were concerned, he was pretty sure nothing was going on beyond the usual feeble plots of landless younger sons and the few who remained alive who opposed his father. These plans rarely came to fruition, and if they became a problem, the heads of the plotters would adorn pikes near the docks as a warning to others. It was a sad truth, he reflected, that treachery was a way of life in the north regardless of oaths taken or the expected loyalty of family members. How often has brother killed brother to get his lands? Wives were known to poison their husbands in order to have her lover supplant him. Uncles killed nephews, and so on. Few indeed were the kings who died in their beds.

There was only one man who was capable of causing him harm in the near run, although he hesitated to tell others of this belief because the fellow was considered an insignificant and cowardly man. This was partially true, for the man was a great coward but hardly inconsequential.

Hugo Bavo, known as *Hugo the Silent*, was the Count of Flanders. As such, he ruled lands that included the lowlands of Frisia to the border of Frankia and many leagues inland. His lands were a mixture of fine farms, swamps, and woodlands; every sort of land could be found except for hills, for the land was flat. The populace was a mixture of tribes and remnants of past migrations. They spoke several tongues, but the ones along the coast spoke the Salt Sea trade language. He had several port cities growing in size and importance as trade centers.

He was called *The Silent* because he never returned urgent messages that appealed to him for military assistance. Those who asked for his aid included both his older brothers, now deceased, his cousin, the King of Frankia, and several invaders who asked him to join in the pillaging of various lands. That is not to say he would refuse to send his troops to battle (without him, of course), but there had to be a sufficient reward to tempt him and a great certainty of success. Bormo had reported that Hubert had strengthened his coastal strongholds and advised his vassals to be diligent in training their men and providing them with weapons. This was significant, the king thought, for Hubert was regarded as being tightfisted in money matters.

He could never understand how such a man could exist; Hubert wouldn't last one Thor's day to the next among the Danes; his corpse would feed the bottom dwellers in the harbor. Bormo claimed that the man was frail, and others thought that he would die sooner than later. Yet he got control of Flanders; when his brothers fought each other, he stayed above the fray, letting them butcher each other. Perhaps the idea of his impending demise was the result of wishful thinking. Perhaps for some perverse reason unfathomable to mortals, the Gods favored him. All he could do was shrug his shoulders at the thought of this spindly man casting his eyes upon the throne of Denmark. It was absurd, but still, he had a niggling sensation that there was more to this Count of Flanders than meets the eye. He would talk with Bormo soon to ensure adequate means were in hand to keep an eye on Flanders.

Such things would no doubt be considered and debated among his counselors. Once in a while, they were able to shed some light on a complicated question. But the one he relied on the most was the one who shared his pillow at night.

Thora Monsdatter was a jarl's daughter from Hordaland who brought much to the marriage in the way of land, money, and possessions. She also brought an extensive knowledge of who was who in the many of the lands fronting the Salt Sea. Her father was an energetic trader who grew rich selling furs, sealskins, walrus hides, and pitch to the Franks, taking grain in payment which he sold to the Danes. While she was at his side, she learned not only the business of trading but also gathered much information about the rulers, jarls, and other important people and their families.

That night he mentioned his worry about the defeated pirates; she had already reached the same conclusion. "Husband," she said, "we can't know for sure what is going on. Not yet, anyway. But I agree that we must keep watch on our neighbors, especially the Cours and the Count of Flanders, who also owns most of Frisia and has estates in Frankia. He is slippery like an eel, and his favorite pastime is counting his money. He has spies, too; one of them is here in Roskilde; Bormo knows who it is, of course. This might be useful in the future if we wish to make Hugo's ears twitch at the lies we send him. But the Cours are getting more dangerous with every passing day. They are a very warlike people who've found that robbing others is a quick way to wealth. Those are the only ones strong enough to challenge us. The Swedes and Geats are busy fighting each other. Someday a strong man will quell these barking dogs and become a High King, but nobody has risen yet. If anything, the situation has gotten worse. The same holds for Scandia; they don't fight as much as the Swedes or Geats, their kingdoms are too small to pose a threat. Nor do these small kingdoms desire to be put under the yoke of some great ruler. Rich men like my father wouldn't like it if they had to pay tribute and taxes to somebody else. The day may come when a man like your father will rise up and make all submit to him, but not for the time being. But it can't be denied that we control the route out of the Salt Sea; none can go in or out save by your leave, husband, and this makes us a target."

"Very true, my love," the king said as he prepared his mind for sleep, "we can only be vigilant and train our forces. Worry won't help, but the pirate gold will help us to be better armed and prepared for the future." With that, the king rolled over and promptly fell asleep. Thora envied his ability to turn off his thoughts and go to sleep quickly; she didn't have that gift. But it did no good to worry, but her husband was right; they needed to be watchful.

Epilogue

I took Astra to the one place in the city where I knew we could be alone, the roof of the North Tower. From here, we could get a splendid view of the harbor. I returned with Jarl Hakon's ships yesterday morning; Astra had been back three days by then.

"Tomorrow is the great feast and celebration. No doubt a song will be ready to commemorate your defeat of the Kraken and the dragon, not to mention the one that people call the *King of the Damned*. I had no idea when I was married that it would be to a renowned warrior."

"No doubt I will have to endure all the praise that the poets can dream up; worse yet, I'll be expected to pay them for it. It seems so unfair that Steinson is not here to see the victory he did so much to make possible," I said as I leaned over the wall to view the harbor.

"He's the one who first suspected that the horrors in Scandia were but a ruse to draw the King out so that, in the meantime, his capital could be sacked and robbed by the pirate conspiracy. They fully accepted the lie, his idea, that was spread about saying that the king was going north in great strength in the first month of the raiding season. But the king's strength went south, where they fought a battle on the coast of the Jutes. The ships sent north were only a raiding party, a powerful one, though, that also contained a magical weapon."

"It was a good thing that the king's ships came upon the pirate ships in the morning," Astra said as we sat down and leaned our backs against the wall, "I can't do anything at night; I have to see the wind blow and the rainfall. We were only a few miles off the coast when we spotted them. The wind had been mild from out of the east; they were going north under oars. Suddenly the wind picked up speed from the north, slowing them to a crawl. They had at least a dozen ships crammed with men but no clue what to do if things turned against them.

"I made sure the wind was strong until we were almost on them, then I let it die. I had an idea of what was to follow, but I had to watch in case I was needed, but it was nothing I'd care to see again.

"Our archers hit them as soon as we were in range, they shot a few arrows at us, but their aim was wild, and nobody was hit. By the time we reached them, some of their warriors were dead or had arrows sticking out of them.

"The sound of the ships colliding, along with the yells of the warriors, was deafening. Then there were the screams of the wounded and dying, and soon there were cries from those drowning. It was horrible beyond belief, sickening, in fact

"Our ship hit a pirate vessel with a glancing blow and got pushed away by the collision, but our men threw ropes with grapples on them and pulled them alongside.

"I can't begin to explain the confusion as shields hit each other and the noise made with axes and swords. They tried to keep from being boarded, but it was hopeless. I saw King Bjornson throw a spear that hit a man so hard that the tip of it stuck out a hand's breadth from his back. They told me later that this man had been the pirate ship's captain. They cut his head off and hung it from the mouth of the dragon on the King's ship.

"But I saw one thing about these pirates, something the others might have been too busy to notice. These men were not all from the north, some were, but many were not. They were too lean and had dark hair like the Franks, their skin was darker, and they fought differently. It's hard to explain, but I just *know* they came from somewhere else." Her words confused me, but I noted it as a subject to remember; at the moment, I was more interested in hearing about the battle.

"Did any escape?" I asked.

"A few ships escaped; they were the ones who saw us first and quickly turned west, making for the open sea; those were the smart ones. As for the rest, they were either sunk or captured. I saw the ship next to us, the one belonging to Jarl Ottson, hit a pirate ship in the middle, crushing the side in. All of them on that ship drowned. As for their men, maybe a hundred or so were captured; to be sold as slaves; four ships were also taken. They must have gotten the pirate gold; I heard a lot of cheering when they looted the captured ships."

"Jarl Hakon says that the pirates don't always take their gold with them. Still, I can't imagine they would want to leave their treasure at home in the care of other thieves. Even among the Danes, that would be dangerous; with robbers like those of the Fang Islands, who swear no oaths, things must be much worse. Did anyone notice when you changed the direction of the wind?" I asked.

"I don't think so; I was careful where I stood. Nobody paid much attention to me. Of course, the King knew; he winked at me later in the day. Most people thought I was just a serving wench if they noticed me. I would be happy if nobody knew, but that isn't possible, is it?"

"No, it isn't," I said, putting my arm around her shoulder. "More people than you know understand your powers, mine also after this adventure with this hanged necromancer and his pet dragon. It probably wasn't his anyway," I said, thinking aloud, "where would he get a dragon? I don't think they're easy to come by."

"It would have to be the Swart dwarfs, then," Astra said as she rested her head on my shoulder. "Dragons are magical creatures. If this man who raised the dead didn't own it, that leaves only the dwarfs. But tell me," she said as she turned slightly to look me in the eye, "was the Kraken real? I don't understand that part of it at all."

"No, it was only a curse. It had about as much reality about it as one of my drawings does; in fact, it burned like parchment."

"Speaking of your drawings, I wonder how they are doing at putting up the village walls? Do you think the King would allow us to go there now that this is done? We won the fight; what more is there to do?"

"There will always be more to do; we should face up to the fact that we are not leaving. Maybe if we ask him quickly, while he is not in a position to refuse us favors, if we could take a quick trip back to the village to settle our affairs. He might well approve it. We have to face facts; this is our home now. We should dispose of our property back in the village and bring everyone here. We are now rich, important, and in danger, of course." At this, she squeezed my hand as I kissed her forehead. "I don't care how much gold we got; I never want to see a battle like this again. The screams were bad enough, but the smell was worse. The stench of blood, vomit, and shit was everywhere. I didn't realize that men when they are killed, shit themselves. Maybe the others didn't notice; maybe I was the only one not filled with battle frenzy. I'm going to be a long time forgetting this."

"I'm fortunate, I guess; I've seen skirmishes but never a real battle, at least when awake; from what you've said, I don't think it would be very pleasurable. A fake Kraken and a real dragon were enough for me."

"The King will want you to raise a stone to commemorate this great victory. Have you given it any thought?"

"Yes, I know what I will put on it. We'll see it again tonight, although now it is going away from us. The hairy star proved lucky for us, not for others."

"That's a good idea," she said as she kissed me, "We can date the beginning of our new life among the Danes by this star."

"All Hail King Baldur Bjornson, Queen Thyra, and the hairy star that he rules by, and the Queen of Storms," I said as I returned her kiss with great energy.

Prologue to Vol. II
The Jutland Cannibal

"That reminds me, in the morning, I must deal with another member of the Jute tribe, the prisoner. What a joy that promises to be."

"If you torture him, do not tell me; I hate to hear about such things. I wouldn't say I like the executions either. I don't care what the court women say about such things."

"The torture will be done to me, I think. I expect the prison to stink and the man to be insane. From what they told me, he begs for human flesh to eat."

Yet when I saw this man the next morning, he seemed tame enough, despite his reported taste for human flesh. It was the first time I had been inside the new prison built hard against the city wall on the side past the barracks. It was small; the Danes were not ones to keep people for great lengths of time, and prisoners awaiting trial were the most common sort, followed by those awaiting public execution. These groups had one thing in common, all such people held had a lean and hungry look about them. The jailers were not given to wasting food on mere prisoners.

This man, whom the guard informed me, went by the name of Skraling, looked better than he did the previous day. He was brought in, unchained, and shoved onto a bench across from me. I gave him a small bottle of mead to drink that I had brought from home. I'm sure this was his first drink outside of water since he was taken captive.

He drank it easily enough, yet I wondered about his wandering eyes. His countenance looked for all the world to be that of a beaten dog.

"Skraling, who are you, and where were you born?" I asked him as his gaze rested on the top of the table in front of him. There was no response whatsoever. I repeated it louder with the same result. Part of me wanted to summon the jailor to give him a good cuff across the face, but I doubted the utility of such an action. Then from my bag, I took out a small loaf I had brought from home and put it in front of him. He grabbed it up from the table and gnawed at it while looking suspiciously at me out of the corner of his eye.

"Tell me about yourself; where were you born?" I asked again.

"I was an Angle until the Jutes burned our village. They took my sister prisoner and me and sold us as slaves. I don't know what happened to the rest. They beat and sold me to the pirates; I worked in their fields and rowed their boats."

"Where did you get the mark on your shoulder?" At this, he looked at his shoulders dumbly and shook his head.

"I don't know," he replied with a shake of his head, "I've never seen it before."

"You're a liar," I said, staring at him, "that has been on you for years."

"Maybe you are right," he said as he turned his head to see the mark, "but I don't remember much about my life like others do; sometimes I have dreams; even when I'm not sleeping, they scare me."

"Dreams, what sort of dreams?" I asked skeptically as I grew impatient with this man's ridiculous lies.

"Dreams you wouldn't want to have," he replied with a slight shudder. "My dreams are never good ones. There are always men fighting, men dying, villages burning, and dead men casting lots."

"The Jutes told us that your home was full of bones and skulls of your victims. How often did you eat men and women? Or did you feast on children? Tell me which you found most to your taste."

"I have never eaten anyone," he said in horror, "I would die before I did such a thing. But why would the Jutes say that? I knew very little of their land until I escaped. I sailed by their lands on a raid, but we were wrecked in a storm. Luckily, I was not chained to the bench as the others were; I was busy bailing water when we hit the reef."

His statements explained a lot if they were true. I decided to prod him with a touch of magic to test his truthfulness to see if I could get a response. I didn't have to wait long for a result; he stiffened as tightly as a strung bow for a minute and gradually relaxed.

"Who is this? A man of magic, I think," said a different voice. He paused for a moment breathing deeply, his nostrils flaring. "Yes, a man of magic who cuts runes for his bread. Yes, he knows things, and yes, he wants to know more. Should I tell him? Does he have a right to know? Maybe not, yet he uses Odin's 12th spell, which is quite rare." This he spoke but in a voice not his own. I was bewildered and wary, although I tried not to show it.

"Who are you? An undead spirit? A ghost? What did you do to this poor man?"

"Why should I tell you, rune cutter? You have paid me no fee. Even farm boys know you must pay a spirit before he gives you any information. Right now, you need information, I think."

This disconcerted me, for I knew nothing of ghosts or their lore among the Danes. That is, if the man I am talking to was really a ghost, not a madman. Yet this person, or spirit, knew a spell of Odin's, which was highly unusual. "If you know that I cut runes, you must know that I have their true power," I said in an even voice, thinking it prudent not to jump to any conclusions at this point.

"Yes, I feel your magic and know something of your mind. You are very unusual. While many can use magic to some extent, there are few indeed who have studied it. Fewer yet who can use it for their purpose as a smith uses a hammer. I think this has been in your family, although I know nothing of your history. A powerful king employs you among the Danes. You have," he continued after some hesitation, "saved his throne by your magic, yet you are not a Dane; very curious. I saw you yesterday at the Thing, not through my own eyes; of course, you sat with the other high lords. Yet you have time to interrogate a mongrel dog sent to you by the Jutes. That is even stranger. Perhaps we can help each other; maybe an agreement can be reached?"

"A deal with one who ate the bodies of the dead? You are either a madman or a malevolent spirit; I'm not sure which is worse. What kind of agreement could I possibly make with you?"

"You doubt me, which is no wonder," mouthed the man sitting in front of me, who now relaxed slightly, "It has been some time since I walked with my own legs, and not another's, upon the sunny fields of my lands. Once, I was a powerful landowner among the Jutes, although my mother was an Angle. I was a warrior too, who fought the Danes twice, being victorious both times. But my brother coveted my lands and my wife, so one warm summer night, he poisoned me. Then as I lay dying, he put a curse on me--one of pure evil. Of course, he gave me a good funeral while all the time laughing at my fate. I was buried in a mound with much in the way of grave goods, including my horse which I rode to Hel. I thought I would join the throng of the dead passing over the bridge, *up north and under,* as they used to say. But as I rode my horse to the bridge, I found my way blocked by the daughter who rules those parts. She told me that I could not pass for the foul stink of the curse laid upon me by my brother. But she felt pity for me as she learned the manner of my death and the battles I had fought bravely while alive. She gave me a task to perform; if I should fulfill it, I could cross the bridge into Hel. This gave me hope as I waited alone in that mound of earth day after day."

"What was the spell that he used to keep you from joining the others in the lands of the departed?" I asked, as my curiosity was now overwhelming.

"It was the spell of the *Dead Man's Legs* which is done by digging up the body of a hanged man and skinning him of his hide from just above the knee downwards. Each leg must be done in one piece. He put them on his own feet just before he killed me. Then, using an iron knife he had stolen from a widow, he made small cuts on my body where they wouldn't be seen. This allowed the dark magic to enter my body."

"So, the trickster's daughter wouldn't have you in her realm. I confess I have not heard of that," I said as I sat there trying to think despite my astonishment. "What task did she put upon you?"

"She must hear the spells known by Odin recited by me in her presence. All of them, according to her, were eighteen in number. Since then, I found twelve, the last being known to you. If you can help me find the rest of them, I will help you."

"I wasn't aware that I needed any help. Yet I must ask how you, as a man without magic, at least while you were alive, came to know *any* of the spells of Odin? Such things are known to few."

"That is true, master of runes; I knew nothing about such things when I walked alive upon the earth. Yet after I had been refused entry across the bridge, I was returned to the mound my body was buried in. There I remained for several years, peering out from time to time, at night or on very dark days, to see the seasons change. One day another dead but restless spirit walked by in the body of another; he sensed me. Walking up to the mound, he called me forth; I could do nothing but obey, for he was a man of magic like yourself, only he too had died and been refused admittance to Hel, why he never said. He shared with me many secrets, including such spells of Odin that he knew. He felt it his duty to share knowledge with me as we were both in a similar circumstance, although I was more miserable than he. He taught me how to leave the earth at night, ride on the backs of animals, and, most importantly, capture a man who walked too close to my grave. If I captured a man, I would live in his body as long as he lived; if he died, I would need to find another."

"Then this unfortunate man came by; you took him like a man might catch a fish."

"Yes, it took two more years, but eventually, a man came walking by at dusk. He was a stranger, for no local man would walk near a barrow at any time, much less at the hour of sunset. He was a dull man, an escaped former slave to the Fang Island pirates. Still, he was better than nothing."

"Let me guess your next move; you tracked down your brother."

"Yes, I did, I admit it," he paused long enough for a sour-sounding laugh, "he was still living although older for more than ten years had passed since I was alive. I strangled him and cut my wife's throat, too, because I'm sure she was part of my murder. I found them both together in my bed. Then I took their bodies by horseback to the shack where my host and I lived, located in a remote part of the forest, yet they eventually tracked me down. Before they came, I sampled the flesh of my late brother and my whore wife. Few things are sweeter than the meat of an enemy long hated. There is much else, of course, but none of it to our profit."

"You have suggested there is something to be gained for me if I help you in some manner. But there is nothing that I want from you, neither gold nor silver or any of your filthy magic."

"Spare me your heat; you speak of what you do not know," here this ghost or corporal apparition leaned forward, folding his hands in front of him, "I know from my time here in your jail and elsewhere that there is a canker eating at the heart of the kingdom. Those who put the mark on this man's shoulder are in your midst. Like a worm inside an apple, they are chewing and chewing, night and day. When you see that the apple has rotted from the inside, it will be too late, your magic notwithstanding."

"You promise me information, yet you have not said what you want for your help."

"I need the remaining spells that Odin knows. I don't need to be able to cast them myself. But I must know their qualities and their names. There are only six that I don't know--six of eighteen. With those, I can cross the bridge. You can travel and meet the people that I cannot. You could do it with your skill and luck; you could find the spells that I lack. If you do, you can save your King, your family, and your own life. For those who plot are men of desperate purpose and skill; should they prevail, none of you will live, don't think either that all the gold held by the pirates has been captured; you didn't take half of it." "If you don't live up to your end of the bargain, what could I do? You are a spirit."

"You could," he replied after some hesitation, "take me far out to sea with a rope around my neck tied to an anchor stone. My spirit would be stuck at the bottom of the sea for a long time. The sharks and crabs would not be good company."

"I will think about it," I replied. This would require thought, yet his words didn't appear to contain falsehoods, at least any that I could detect. As for the treasure of the pirates, he could well be right.

"Your time is your own; for now, I must withdraw, for contact with the living tires me; you can have your slave back."

I was confounded by the conversation that I had with the prisoner. Or I could say the talk I had with the two people who inhabited that single body. To say that I was skeptical of this tale would be an understatement. Yet if it was a lie, then to what end? To waste the time of a court drudge? That seemed doubtful; the kingdom would remain the same if I died in the next hour. Did he wish to cause us harm by accusations of disloyalty among the King's counselors? This, too, seemed doubtful; the King could always find new advisers. Yet I know truth when I hear it, and if the danger was real, I had to act; the world knows what happens to kingdoms that fall. There would be a great slaughter and no end of privations. The rich kingdom of the Danes would be a land of paupers and burned barns. But how would I find the missing spells of Odin? Was it even possible?"

Suggested Further Reading

The Anglo-Saxon Chronicle, 1912, translated by the Rev. James Ingram, E. P. Dutton & Co. London. Written in the 9th century by a scribe in Wessex, it's the annals of the Saxons from the time of the invasion of Julius Caesar to the reign of Alfred the Great.

The Poetic Edda, The 1908 version by Olive Bray, is available online and in many printed forms. The original 13th-century author who collected these stories is unknown other than he was probably a high churchman. This work is the most extensive and probably the most reliable of all the early Icelandic and Norse sources. Available online.

The Prose Edda by Snorri Sturluson, 1179-1241, was a historian and politician who collected and edited Icelandic Norse mythology and heroic stories from a Christian perspective. His work is open to interpretation, and he has suffered extensively at the hands of modern scholars.

The History of the Danes by Saxo Grammaticus, who is thought to have been a 13th-century churchman. He gathered folk tales and sagas, some of which vary considerably from the Icelandic sources. Eric Christiansen's translation is the most modern. The sagas collected in the Eddas often differ substantially from this source.

A History of the Vikings, Gwyn Jones, Cambridge University Press, too many editions to count. A great book at any level, highly recommended for further reading.

The Saga of the Volsungs translated and edited by Jackson Crawford. 2017 Hackett Publishing. The author is probably the greatest living scholar of the Old Norse Language, and his many lectures available on YouTube are a must for anyone who wants to understand the old Norse culture.

Egil's Saga, Penguin Classic, 2004. Story of the life and times of Egil Skallagrimsson, who was a 10th-century poet, farmer, warrior, and psychopath. His story is a popular one because he is such a strangely gifted person who had a lot of talent besides some very disturbing personal traits.

About the Author
Robert Peterson

Originally from Wisconsin, he now makes his home in Florida with his cat, Arthur. He's a lifelong student of Norse culture and history with a particular interest in Icelandic sagas and early runes. A hobby of his for many years is the collection of artifacts from the neolithic sub-Saharan culture of N. Africa.

Made in the USA
Coppell, TX
17 May 2025